GW00994489

The writing of Elizabeth Berrid̶̶ broadcast both in Britain and abroad. She has been well received by the critics on both sides of the Atlantic and in 1964 gained the Yorkshire Post Literary Award for *Across the Common* which was subsequently serialised by the BBC. Her other novels include *House of Defence*, which was translated into French, Portuguese and Spanish, *Be Clean, Be Tidy* and *Upon Several Occasions*, also serialised by the BBC.

Her activities have included journalism, broadcasting, criticism and several television plays, in addition to a three year spell in publishing on both the editorial and publicity sides. Married with a grown up son and daughter, she divides her time between London and the country, which she says is the ideal way of getting the best of both worlds.

Elizabeth Berridge

ACROSS THE COMMON

First published in Great Britain by
William Heinemann Ltd, 1964
Published in Abacus by
Sphere Books Ltd 1985
30–32 Gray's Inn Road, London WC1X 8JL
Copyright © Elizabeth Berridge, 1964

Printed and bound in Great Britain by
Cox & Wyman Ltd, Reading

For Graham, with love

Time present and time past
Are both perhaps present in time future . . .

But to what purpose
Disturbing the dust on a bowl of roseleaves
I do not know . . .

(from *Burnt Norton*
by T. S. Eliot)

ONE

I KNEW IT was finished, so I finished it myself. One day when Max was at the art school I packed my things, did all the washing and ironing, checked the mending and tidied his drawers. Then I cooked ahead for three days, took a purple pill and under its influence was able to write some sort of crazy note. He didn't know I had these pills; he thought I was too stable to need them. But if he couldn't take the Braithwaites, then I couldn't take him. It was simple. Hadn't the aunts said: 'If you ever want to leave that man, come home'? They always called any man not a relative, 'that man'. They would put me in the room where I had slept as a child; it had been waiting for me for years. It was big and sunny and it overlooked the common.

So I did just that. I went by train to Pagham Green and walked across the common to the house that had been home to me until I ran away with Max twelve years before. The aunts stood at either side of the front door, without surprise, and embraced me in the intense, dry way of the elderly. Then Gibby came out of the kitchen, bringing an extra plate, an extra knife and fork. It was supper-time.

My grandfather had built the house in the eighties. It was tall and big and excelled in useless crenellations; in the front an immense stretch of holly hedge gave the house its name. At the back it had a long garden that ran right down to the edge of the common, but was separated from it by a high wall and an iron gate, now invisible behind dense blackberry bushes. In those long, hot days at the turn of the century, this had been the country. Lying south of the river, in one of the loops, beyond Clapham, cornfields had stretched between the new houses and the church; country lanes had turned between nut hedges. The new station, with its geraniums and its infrequent trains up to Victoria, had been hailed by some residents and bitterly regretted by others who had come to Pagham Green to retire to clean air and peace. Each of the new prosperous houses was topped by an individual folly; my grandfather had built a tower on his, with a square look-out. As a child I had gazed over to the far south, past Richmond and places I could not then name (and had now forgotten), to the South Downs, miles away. I liked to see the smoke rolling up from the long chimneys of invisible factories in between us and the scoured downs, and listen to the far-off hoot of the sirens.

'That's where they make wooden pips for raspberry jam,' my mother had once said. 'Don't ever eat bought jam, pet. They make it out of mashed turnips and old apples and colour it with cochineal. Then they put the pips in.' I thought about sackfuls of wooden pips being emptied into huge vats stirred by sweating men in holland overalls using long broom-handles, like our washerwoman, Mrs Priestley, who stirred the bubbling sheets in the boiler in the scullery.

I remembered this particularly, because my mother did not live long after that to tell me other things to guard against. And when, years later, I ate a raspberry jam tart in an ABC with Max and bit hard on a pip, I at once felt my mother's silk sleeve flicking against my face as we stood together, her arm around my shoulder, high up on that look-out tower, the cool night breeze flattening our skirts against our legs, on a level with the restless tree-tops. In those days the tall chimneys were part of another life, sentinels over all the mean houses which, although I did not know it, were even then creeping towards us over the fields and up the long hill past the red, hidden asylum.

·   ·   ·   ·   ·

The aunts asked no questions, for to them a return was normal: it was departure they could not bear. They did not ask me how Max was, for it was evident that had he been ill I would not be there. He was alive, in his world and not in theirs, and they were thankful. We talked about their difficulties and their failing eyesight and how impossible it was to get a boy to help in the garden. Since old George's death, it was getting beyond Aunt Seraphina.

'I'll help,' I said. 'I love gardening.'

They looked at their plates. They had lived together for so long that it was unnecessary for them to exchange meaning looks. Thoughts flowed freely between them, as if they were enclosed by another element. This one I picked up without effort. Does she mean to stay long, then?

'I'd like to stay for several weeks, if I may,' I said. 'I haven't seen you for a long time.'

Aunt Rosa said, ringing for Gibby to clear away, 'Your Aunt Cissie is coming to stay for a while, dear. You know she has had this operation on her hip and she needs rest. That hotel she insists on living in is no good, no good at all. They don't understand that people need care after an operation. We shall be most grateful for your help.'

Aunt Rosa was the eldest. It was she who made decisions.

The door opened and the trolley was wheeled in. This, I noticed, had only recently replaced the heavy butler's tray that usually stood by the sideboard, and it was odd to see Gibby's tiny figure behind it. I supposed that she was now too old to manage a heavy tray. 'I'll wash up, Gibby,' I said, not wanting to be treated as a guest. 'Shouldn't you be going home?'

Silence. Then Gibby looked at me and adjusted her wig. She still thought nobody knew it was a wig, and accepted compliments on the black sheen of her hair with complaisance. It sat awkwardly above her wrinkled face like a new sheet-iron roof on a weathered cottage.

'Bless you, you're out of date, Miss Lou,' she grumbled, pursing her lips and beginning to collect the plates. 'I live here now. Got your old playroom at the top. Didn't they tell you? My Fred passed on at Christmas. I 'ad the pensions people after me, and the Welfare wanting me to move to a new council flat. They're pullin' down our road, see, and I 'ad to get out. Interferin' woman came and made remarks, so Miss Rosa said—'

'I thought I'd written and told you,' interrupted Aunt Seraphina, turning her napkin in her nervous hands. 'I'm sure I wrote and told you—'

'We must have written, dear,' repeated Aunt Rosa. 'Yes, I'm —'

Gibby went on as if they had not spoken, piling dishes on to the trolley. 'Places goin' up like beanstalks in the Lane,' she said. 'Give me the verticles just to see 'em. "You're not goin' to stick me up in the sky at my age," I said to 'em. "I'm not a blinkin' star. I'm a sight too old to twinkle," I told 'em, so —'

'Don't forget we're having coffee in the drawing-room this evening,' said Aunt Rosa firmly. 'You can tell Louise all about it tomorrow.'

For a moment the two old women looked at one another, then authority and habit won, and Gibby twitched a half-wink at me as I opened the door for her to pass through with the laden trolley.

'She does go on so about those flats, poor old thing,' said Aunt Rosa, sighing. 'It was a great shock, a great shock. One doesn't care to have one's home pulled down, no, terrible; although, of course, they were rabbit hutches. Rabbit hutches in Parrot Lane, and —'

'Oh, I loved her house! I used to go there to tea often, do you remember? Poor Gibby . . . and losing Fred as well —'

'It isn't easy to be old, Louise, in her position. I suppose

4

she's lucky to have us. But she's so obstinate. She wouldn't tell the pensions people her correct age, so she's only just got her old age pension. I had to interview them myself.' Aunt Rosa smiled, almost cannibalistically. In her sweet plump way she could make mincemeat of officious persons. 'Anyway, she's better off now than she's ever been, poor old soul.'

'Not so much of the poor old soul, Rosa,' broke in Aunt Seraphina sharply. 'You can only give her a few years. Of course, she's very slow,' she went on, turning to me. 'But in this great house, it's nice to have someone about. That's why it's so nice to have you, dear. And Cissie, of course. It will be company, quite like old times.'

'Cissie will have papa's study,' Aunt Rosa said, ignoring her. 'She certainly can't manage the stairs, and we can't lift her wheelchair up them.'

'Wheelchair?'

'You've been out of touch,' flashed Aunt Seraphina, with one of her bitter, challenging looks. 'You haven't been near us for nearly a year, otherwise you would know that your Aunt Cissie broke her hip running across the road at Eastbourne. She never walks where she can run, *as* you know. She's been in hospital for four months, and the bone hasn't set properly – how can you expect it to, at her age? So she's in a wheelchair.'

'She's never out of it,' added Aunt Rosa, 'except to go to bed, of course.'

'*And* never will be, whatever they tell her at the hospital.'

This rapid crossfire of information and implied reproach unnerved me and I found myself saying defensively that Max and I had been in Ireland, arranging an exhibition. Rather lamely, in the face of their uncomprehending silence, I finished, 'What bad luck for her.'

'Bad luck! This family has had nothing go right for it since —' Was I imagining it, or did she hesitate for a fraction of a second as Aunt Rosa looked at her, 'Oh, since mama died.'

I dreaded the arrival of my third aunt. The news of her coming clouded my curious homecoming. It somehow dulled the dramatic edge of what, to me at least, was a mysterious reappearance. Aunt Cissie had the same effect on me as a lemon was supposed to have if sucked in front of an unfortunate trombonist. She dried up my juices. Her whole life had disbelief as its pivot and for this reason I had always been wary of her. Once, years ago, she had been recklessly, dogmatically sure of herself. She would argue with the wry humour of the convinced, a person on the right side of life. Since the war, which had robbed her of her second husband and her only son, something had shifted in her. A new, unbalanced cynicism revealed itself by a sarcastic twist of the mouth, a semi-quaver of a shrug. Nothing, now, could move her. She would have turned the pages of Nero's music, one felt (had he had any), whilst he fiddled, glad of the light of the flames. At seventy she believed in nothing but her own and other people's wickedness. No, I did not look forward to Aunt Cissie's arrival. She had never admired me.

After supper the aunts' extreme tactfulness drove me to bed early. Three people sitting in a large drawing-room drinking small cups of coffee in unaccustomed formality, tossing small talk from one to the other, each determined to avoid the unfortunate leading question, was a strain. We had known each other too intimately for too long, and yet not at all. All we had in common was the past. I could meet them as a child, but not as a woman, and they were strange to me. Surely the prodigal son had had doubts that first night at home?

I began, for the first time that day, to doubt my decision.

6

There was no bedside lamp in my room. This was to discourage reading in bed: the journey over the cold lino-leum to the light switch by the door was, they hoped, a deterrent to a bad habit. But I saw that Gibby had laid out my nightdress by the white poodle with its zipped-up back, and the narrow brass bed with its cold white candlewick cover emphasized the schoolgirl purity of my former state. I had grown used to bright blankets and cheap bright rugs and abstract canvases on the walls, and this bare room struck a chill. The only picture in it was a large pale watercolour of two children crouching together, half in and half out of bed with a mouse looking up at them. Underneath was written, 'What is the good of a Perfect Day, If you can't have a Perfect Night?' I never knew who painted it, but it was evidently 'after' Mabel Lucy Attwell.

Max had not telephoned, but perhaps that was too much to expect. Was he in bed? More, was he alone? I hoped he had eaten some of the apple pie I had left for him.

The effects of the purple pill had worn off hours ago and I put down my deflated feeling to this. The trees rustled out-side in the garden, and reminded me that this was of course the wrong season for the magnolia tree. In the spring moon-light it glowed with a white translucence as if quicksilver ran in its veins instead of sap. Instead, as I looked out now, it spread its leaves darkly under the high, bleached moonlight of late summer, which lay over the garden and the common equally, boldly blocking in shadows of tree and shrub. It was very quiet. In the Bayswater flat we had to shut the windows against the noise of traffic. It wasn't true to say that one became accustomed to noise, especially if one lived near traffic lights. All the same, here, in the near-country, my own thoughts deafened me.

I was nearly asleep when Aunt Seraphina came in. She was in her long summer dressing-gown and the flowers on it looked black in the white light from the uncurtained

7

windows. She half-drew the curtains against that strong light, fearing moon madness. Her hair was brushed long over her shoulders, grey and fine, and her face looked smaller on the long wrinkled neck. A withered bud, a frosted rose on a long stem. Circe in decline.

She looked at me, hesitated, but did not come to kiss me. At the door she turned, asked quietly, 'I would like to know the real reason for this visit, Louise.'

Just as quietly I replied, secure in my childhood room looking up at that tree-patterned ceiling, remembered yet strange, telling her the truth, too tired not to. 'I want to know why my marriage has failed. This is where I can find out.' And went to sleep surprised at myself, for the truth is not a courtesy the young often extend to the old.

TWO

'MAX,' I SAID, waking to the strange morning, wanting to share this dream of being in a room I had known from childhood, a room into which a man had never come, 'have you noticed,' I said clearly in sleep, 'how sexless some rooms are? I dreamed I was in a nursery, but it could have been an old woman's room, it —'

The words became meaningless, lost their shape like flames in sunlight, trailed among bunches of faded purple grapes and green leaves on the walls, moved as in a nightmare, puffed out. I put a hand behind my head, caught hold of a brass rail. So Max was the dream. He faded as I spoke his name, and the sound of it in my ears, against the curious outside silence, woke me up.

White linen curtains clattered back on brass rings and the morning sprang in. Gibby stood by my bed with a cup of tea and some thin biscuits, nicely arranged on a tray.

'I'm not ill, Gibby,' I said at once, sitting up, full of guilt. 'What's the time?'

'Half past seven. Breakfast's at half past eight. If you're not ill, then what do you look like when you're well? Peaky, she is, I said to them, told them straight. That child's peaky. Husband trouble, I expect.'

I sipped my tea, pretending to be sleepy.

'Not that I'm askin', mind. Doesn't do. All the same,' she went on, from the door, 'just remember, Miss Lou. *I've* been married; *they* haven't. I don't count Miss Rosa, poor thing. You might say that was nothing but church-door to coffin, if you ask me. So if you're in trouble —'

She stood hopefully. But I shook my head. The indefinable pressure of the day had already started. Even here I wasn't free of it.

'I just wanted a change. Wanted to see them again. I'm sorry about Fred, Gibby. Was he ill long?'

As she told me about Fred and the hospital, what she had said to the doctor, and how her son Nigel had come to sit by his dad, I knew that this was what I needed. A touch of the real world, a world where people lived and died without pretension, and took one another for granted. Her story was as comforting as a bedtime story told to a child. Her voice had run through my childhood and I never wanted it to stop. When at last she went away satisfied, I told myself that change was the only thing we all feared, and got up to see what changes I would find.

After breakfast I walked across the common, to the shops. The evening before, whilst crossing it, nothing had registered. I had been walking like a shut telescope.

Coming out of the tradesmen's entrance half-way down the cut between the long brick wall of our garden and the equally long and mellow one of the vicarage, I saw that nothing had changed. The square notice on the gate, now almost indecipherable: *No canvassers, no hawkers, no circulars*, still put its ineffectual embargo on the uninvited. There was still the metal post to stop cyclists charging through from the road to the common. The enormous chestnut was bigger, its leaves on the turn like the season itself, its boughs rich with ripening conkers. Here, between the walls, you belonged nowhere. The cut was neutral, between two opposed territories. As a child I had felt the subtle change as I walked along it each day, accompanied either by Gibby or Aunt Seraphina, to my first kindergarten. At one end, the hushed inhabitedness of the mellowed road, the big houses stunned into sleep behind their high hedges and flowering trees; and all remembered time was summer, when men came to resurface the road, and the rich black spreading tar and hot headiness of privet and philodelphus and newly cut grass added to the safety of belonging. I knew the tradesmen's horses, munching in their nosebags as they waited. The milkman's horse, with her curled grey moustache. 'That comes from eating furze,' the milkman had told me, stroking his own well-thatched upper lip. Then, seeing my questioning frown, 'Furze is gorse to you. Nell and me have it for our suppers.' When I relayed this strange remark to Gibby, she had merely said. 'Take no notice. He's Irish. Tongue's so long it'll tie him in knots one day.' And the boys on bicycles, delivering things; meat or groceries or papers – swooping along the newly made surface, with tar and gravel frosting their wheels, crunching and whirring in arcs, with a noise like cornflakes, detachedly whistling. . . .

But the other world was always there. Now I walked quickly, anticipating it, quickening to it with the old excitement. Once the common had spread to a child's horizon; hummocky, boiling with rabbits, sprawling with blackberry bushes, clumps of gorse, yellow and popping; secret with groves of old trees, hawthorn and willow, and sudden dipping ponds. It flowed along the bottom of the long gardens and around the new housing estates that had eaten into it on the southern edges, gouged out of bracken and rough grass. To me, a place for flying kites, for hide-and-seek, for tracking. To the aunts, a place to be feared, lawless as Hounslow Heath in the eighteenth century. They never crossed it unless they went together, and then only by daylight. I was only allowed to play there within sight of the house and with children they knew, and many a time Gibby had been sent to summon me in to meals, standing at the end of the cut and swinging a large brass dinner-bell, like a ship's captain gone mad.

Now I stepped out on to the common and smelt the aftermath of rain. It was a good smell of earth and grass and gorse. Above, the sky was the innocent blue of childhood, and at once I was a child on my way to 'pay the books', a Saturday duty. Then I had walked fast, full of importance, feeling the purse and the weekly account-books hard against my stomach, in a special pocket sewn inside my coat. The aunts had never allowed me to carry money in an outside pocket, sowing seeds of nervousness that still persisted; for it might be stolen, and then where would you be? One never knew what might happen on the common. Other people, who did not possess the Braithwaite code, walked there. Keep to the paths, dear. Avoid the bushes. If you see a man loitering, run. Never, on any account, speak to a stranger. Not even if he were ill? Suppose he wanted to know the time? Never. He would not be ill, he would be drunk, and there is the church clock beyond the trees.

How strange. I thought I had forgotten all that. But perhaps only forgotten things are the real memories – the only ones worth remembering – lying deeper than memory can dredge up. What else would the past yield, fresh from a patient re-living? I stopped by a hawthorn tree, its trunk still as shiny and rubbed from climbing as when our small gang had made it a 'dare' tree. I looked up. The topmost branch, the 'dare' branch, was only a couple of feet above my head. So much for aspiration. Still, I could not resist swinging myself up, dwarfing the tree and my childish self as I did so. From this height the common looked tired, used. White fluff from the tall black poplars (or were they wych elms? I never could learn the names of trees) scattered on the grass. Did children still use it to stuff dolls' pillows?

Why on earth had I come back?

Why had I said that to my aunt last night? How could it possibly help? Max would say it was a bolt-hole; everyone had such a place. One played the game mockingly, 'And what is *your* symbol of security?'

A potting-shed, a teddy bear, a peach, the smell of singeing flannel or a nursery fireguard, drawn curtains. . . . The list changed from person to person.

I was in search of no such thing. I did not want to rediscover the child's world for itself, I only wanted to remember it in order to remember something else, like turning the cut-glass top of a decanter bottle to the sun, to catch the sudden prismatic dazzle. This something lay with the aunts; it was an unease that spoiled relationships, a strange Braithwaite ambience that lay like fall-out over the family.

I walked on, along the path, soberly, a stranger, belonging only on this shrunken, balding common. In the butcher's shop Mr Baines greeted me.

'Haven't seen you for a long time. My, you've got your mother's look!' He was reproachful. I had failed him, growing up to look like my mother. It reminded him of her death, his age. Resentfully he bent to cut the chops. He was nearly bald, his hair reduced to a fine fuzz like that of a monk who had lost his nerve half-way through the creation of a tonsure. His hands were still steady, and his striped apron stretched like another grubby skin over his belly. 'There, that's how they like 'em,' he said, and bent the flaps over and around each bone, calling out the price to the new girl behind her window at the back of the shop. 'Keeping well, are they? Good, good,' and nodded me away.

I moved along the row of shops like a dreamer in a largely alien landscape. Certain things were familiar, familiar enough to lull the dreamer into a sense of false security, so that she does not wake up screaming. The church hall seemed unchanged, with its dirty brick walls and its blistered door; the wool shop, *Mrs Meredith* written above in flowing faded gilt; cards of plastic thimbles and paper books of patterns, large nappy-pins and a discreet notice, half hidden: 'Bust supports made to measure.' What would happen if I went in and ordered one? Dear Miss Meredith (for the *Mrs* was a courtesy title only), was she still alive? Would she remember making my party frocks – the difficult ones that Aunt Seraphina couldn't manage? I paused, my hand on the door, then, a coward, walked on. Too much past at a time was not good for one.

I walked on with the smell of Miss Meredith's dusty hair in my nostrils, for it had wafted up to me as she knelt, her mouth full of pins, fixing a hem; those clever, busy little hands, moulding material into dresses, the whirr of the foot-pedal machine in her head day and night. Dresses had to hang in the air for a day or two, Aunt Seraphina told me, after they had been delivered, to get rid of what she called 'the Meredith mustiness'.

But now the change. I had been lulled enough. Expecting the grocer's to be unchanged, half aware already of the sawdust smell of dried figs in sacks, and of Mr O'Connor's red head bobbing over boxes of Spiller's Shapes, I saw a supermarket. It blared on the corner, hysterical with bargains, and the doors whined open with a hiss. Piles of plastic buckets marked Half Price toppled near the pavement. Plastic baskets. Polythene jugs. Indestructible. No longer was it change and decay in all around I see, the vicar's favourite hymn. Plastic did not decay. Unlike us, it did not contain the seed of its own disintegration.

This upset me, and I set off home, betrayed. Then, half-way across the common, I had to sit down and hunt for an Ephedrin tablet. It was absurd, sitting there near the black poplars, on a new corporation seat, panting like a dog. I couldn't help laughing. Asthma had made my childhood difficult and chancy, but I had thought to outwit it with age. At least with Max I could. Even now I heard his voice, calm and slow. 'In, out. In, out. Breathe from the stomach. Relax. Again. You'll be all right.'

The tablet was bitter on my tongue, swallowed without water. I waited for it to take effect. In time the iron band would loosen and my heart stop pumping like a mad robot. My hands on the seat slats were clammy with strain, so I eased them. This was the sort of panic against which Max protected me, and for the first time since walking out of our flat (could it have been only yesterday?) I realized what I had done. It was worse than being left alone in the dark, unable to breathe, unable to call out. And it was then that I felt the presence of the common, gathered ready to spring. Just as the aunts did, I felt it was hostile.

I had a recurring dream about the common, and always wakened in a sweat after some pursuit. Now I concentrated, trying to recapture that dream, in order to forget the present fear of gradual suffocation. The common was always deserted, and I was walking home from school. Bushes, trees, long summer grasses and a slanting sun. Then, on a seat near the cut, two people sitting. Old people, a man and a woman. As I passed, the old man put out a foot, casually. A long, cracked, unclean, brown boot. I tripped; they got up. I began to run, knowing they were coming after me with no noise. With the illogic of panic, I ran right up to the high garden wall along the bottom of our garden, but a deep ditch filled with nettles and elder bushes deterred me. The gate set in the wall was in any case locked, doubly reinforced by blackberry bushes. There was no way in, although I believed that it would magically open if I said the right word. This word I never remembered. The sun, in this dream always setting, caught the steep side of the conservatory my grandfather had built on to the wall between the first and second storeys of the house, to be reached by an iron spiral stairway, and the red reflection seemed to beckon. The obstacles were too many; I must turn back, dodge past the horrible couple and run up the cut to the other gate, scream for Gibby, sob my way back into safety.

Then the dream varied. If I was half awake, I made it end by pushing the old man aside and running up the cut, into the side gate and so into the garden. If I were too deeply en-meshed, the woman stood across the cut, by the metal post, her big hands spread wide as if to catch tiddlers, smiling quite gently. Then I would wake up, only then, my shout a mere dribble of fear escaping my lips like a moan, like a balloon which stayed the size of a blister for all the effort one put into the blow. The last time I had had this dream Max had heard, or sensed, the dream shout, and I awoke to his arm around me, and the light by the bed switched on.

The common was deserted now, used-looking, and it was midday in September. I was a grown woman, married, strong. My shadow had never lain so long across the grass. To steady myself I thought next about Max.

He was – no, he *is* – a big, loving man. He flows out to people. He is like nectar to those ragged butterflies at the art school where he teaches graphic arts, and they sip from him voraciously, as I had done. 'Though your friend be as sweet as honey, do not lick him away.' Where had I heard this? But no one can lick Max away. He has the strength of a man sure of himself, a man renewed by giving; the source of great waters. I have seen people, especially young people, attach themselves to him like burrs. They drift towards him like those airborne feathery seeds in country lanes, coming to rest against his jacket, holding fast with almost invisible hooks. He is too unregarding to pull them off. I had done the same, and stayed longer.

Twelve years is a long time when you say it. A lot can happen. It is the time between twenty and thirty-two; eight or nine children can be born to a couple, coming singly. Governments and hemlines can rise and fall, the nuclear tests lose their horror through familiarity. It can change an elderly person into a senile one, push a neurotic over the edge into psychosis. Hundreds of supermarkets can be built and the face of a city utterly changed. Species of rare plants and animals can vanish in that time. One artist can find himself, another realize slowly that he is limited, and that the pot of gold at ambition's end is not for him. This had happened to Max, and I resented it for him, because he did not resent it for himself. Resentment was wasteful. He tried to make me see that he had another way, a teacher's way. He gave me examples from nature, like a kind teacher. He drove me mad with his patience, telling me to think of the prodigality of seed that trees and plants and fishes produced, and how small a number actually lived to produce more trees and plants and fishes.

'You'll quote me the parable of the sower next!' I snapped back once. But he had merely smiled. At last he had said, reluctantly, that I'd better think over my real reasons for resenting his lack of worldly success. If I thought deeply enough I'd see that it wasn't for him, but for myself. I wanted the reflection of success, like so many women; it was a quicker way than having to work at something for yourself. I concluded from this that he was baiting me for my inability to produce a child. But that wasn't why I left him.

It wasn't Frankie, either. She was the latest young thing to come to rest against him. A first-year student, thin, insecure, with dark, fine hair that blew long and dead straight across her pointed face. She could do without food and sleep, it seemed, so long as she could be near Max. She could even be nice to me, and offer to clean up the flat and darn Max's socks. She moved in for a time after my last miscarriage and took care of me.

He tolerated her as he tolerated all his students; was

endlessly available. Would discuss anything with them, becoming what they most wanted: mother, father, God. Lover? I wasn't sure. For they all fell in love with him some time or other, usually in their first year. It was the shock of meeting someone who spoke their language, thought their thoughts and was willing to listen, then tossed back their own ideas in more coherent form. I used to lie back on our old blue-velvet divan and watch them all as they speared bits of cheese and toasted it in front of the fire. Our rooms were always crowded with young men and women who never seemed to know any home other than ours. Someone always seemed to be sleeping in a chair, or strumming quietly on a guitar, or bringing in records, or just sitting on the floor reading. Talk and smoke wreathed up, and I would go to sleep, wake up again, and then find they had all gone, and Max was making love to me in a suddenly empty room. I could never fully respond, because I always felt that someone lingered outside; someone was shut out, wanting to come in and share even this with us.

It was this hunger I sensed most about Frankie. Sometimes, going to meet Max, I would find him surrounded. Boys, their long thin legs in black or blue jeans, wild-eyed, bright-shirted, fierce and sullen at the same time. The girls seemed to have broken open their mothers' chests in the attics. One girl wore a lace fichu over a black sweater, topping a black satin skirt, long and full, with bells and sequins sewn round the hem. I never saw her face; her hair covered it like the lifeless dry moss one scraped off a log. Max said, 'She'll be terribly conventional next week. Then, again, she'll go in for jeans and try to pinch one of my shirts. It doesn't hurt. It's good for them. They're striding ahead by experiment. They need absolute freedom if they're to develop. They're only painting themselves like young Indian braves, to give themselves confidence. It's protective colouring.'

'You enjoy them. You belong to them. They mean more to you than your own painting!'

'Of course. Otherwise I couldn't teach them. Thank God I've found my right vocation.'

'Go on, then. *Be* a bloody saint. I don't care.'

He never argued. He raised one eyebrow slightly. He understood, and this drove me mad. It is terribly undermining to be understood, to have allowances made. I am too much of a Braithwaite, and the Braithwaites never make allowances. They never attempt to understand anyone outside their own clan.

It was the Braithwaites, my mother's family, who came outside Max's indulgence. They filled him with a kind of detached horror. He was ruthless about them. Is ruthless. For he blames them for everything awry in me – the asthma particularly.

'They're rock,' he would say. 'Rock. You'll batter yourself to death on them. Keep away, now you've escaped.'

He made a terrible fuss whenever they sent for me to look after one or other of them after their operations. They always had operations: a kidney, or a cataract removed, an unmentionable hysterectomy.

'The Three Grey Women,' he said once after a visit. 'I expected them to pass round the one eye between them. I felt like Perseus.'

'You're heartless. You only have time for the young; not the old.'

'Perhaps you're right.' He would have to think about this. And while he was thinking, I thought, too. By mocking at the Braithwaites he made nonsense of my whole life before I met him. I didn't like being in a no-man's-land.

So perhaps that's why I left him.

When I got home, rather later than they expected, Aunt

19

Seraphina told me that 'that man' had telephoned. He had merely said, when told I was there, but out:

'I only wanted to know where she was. Thank her for leaving everything so tidy.'

Then he had rung off. There was no message.

THREE

I WAS TWO years old when my mother and father came to live at The Hollies and, looking back now, it must have seemed to them like some kind of defeat. Aunt Rosa had also returned, after her brief marriage and early widowhood. 'The boys', as my uncles were always referred to, had left for good, were either dead, or abroad or married. These latter came back with their families for visits, especially at Christmas, when the house was full of aunts, uncles and cousins.

By that time The Hollies was no longer a country house. Pagham Green was becoming a suburb; an outer one, but a suburb all the same. My grandfather did not live to see the snaking concrete roads, nor to hear other people's gramophones or wirelesses over hedges as thick and affluent as his own. He did not know about the tennis courts that succeeded croquet lawns, nor watch stables give way to garages. (My Uncle Bertie owned one of the first electric Mercedes and kept it in the stableyard where my grandmother's barouche had once stood.)

It was a household of women when we arrived, and it went on being so. My grandmother, Aunt Rosa and Aunt Seraphina were the resident goddesses, and they kept the house like a temple, clean and airy and prepared for any other Braithwaite who wished to return. The Hollies was surely, as in the words of the psalmist 'a house of defence', a sanctuary. The household gods were placated with polish and flowers, and in my childhood it seemed that they smiled on us. It never occurred to me, in those days, to question why we were here, rather than in a house of our own. It was accepted that my mother was delicate and that looking after a child and an ailing husband was beyond her. She should never have had a child, my aunts told her. My father was what they called 'chesty', a remarkable understatement that covered anything from asthma or bronchitis to the extremes of tuberculosis, and he made no objection when my grandmother suggested that we should move into The Hollies until, as she put it, he had 'found his feet'. Alas, he never found his feet, for an influenza epidemic killed him when I was eight years old, as it did my mother; they died within a week of each other.

Aunt Seraphina became the centre of my world then. She passionately interested me. I would watch her darting about the house in one of her high states of excitement, absolutely absorbed in her pursuit of the moment. Perhaps this was the reason: absolute absorption is rare in adults; absolute enjoyment even rarer. Alone among my aunts she respected a child's privacy, and for this I loved her. She was always in a state of innocent astonishment, which filled my grandmother in her tart old age with tolerant amusement. As a young girl, she had always had an urge to look after anything alive – plant, child or animal – anything that grew or changed. She was not interested in static things, like furniture or floors or cooking. Perhaps because a soufflé, however perfectly cooked, could not respond. It could only be eaten. Aunt Seraphina responded to everything about her, and demanded a great deal of response in return. Sometimes, disloyally, I found this exhausting, for I was not by nature an exclamatory child. In fact, expeditions did not affect me at all until I had thought about them afterwards, enacted them with my dolls, or told my father about them. She had greatly annoyed my father once by calling me 'Wooden-face', after a visit to the Tower of London.

'She had nothing to say, Gordon, even in poor dear Raleigh's room, even as we paced the walk where *he* had paced! And the ravens might have been sparrows!'

'I liked the dog with the money-box on its back, Aunt Seraphina, I liked that dog. I gave it a penny!'

I was heartbroken at letting her down, and could not understand why I had so displeased her. My father's laughter as she went away, crying, 'But that was on Victoria Station! That was just a *dog*!' had echoed down the years to me, and after his death the memory of it gave me some sort of perspective. He had laughed, not at me, but at her. And after that I think we understood one another better.

Aunt Rosa, to keep her independent status after her husband's early death, had insisted on going into partnership with a friend of his mother's. They ran an agency which supplied governesses and lady's companions to well-to-do families all over the world. The agency insisted on a larger salary from overseas royalty, holding the view that English-women, by virtue of their nationality alone, should be compensated for having to leave their native land and live among a coloured, backward people, who although rich and well-born in their own country, could scarcely be considered the equal in breeding and consequence of a clergy-man's daughter from Warwickshire. This work brought my aunt a great deal of pleasure as well as profit and through it she met various members of the aristocracy, whose crested letters she brought home for us to see. This harmless snobbishness gave us all a great deal of satisfaction and, as she kept in touch with her clients, she had a certain amount of inside information about ducal establishments in London and the country. Sometimes, at week-ends, elevated by a conversation with a duchess, she would bring home orange-flavoured chocolate as a treat, or peaches in brandy from Fortnum's, an echo of that luxury into which she made occasional forays. In all, she brought into The Hollies something of the outside world, she dressed well, and always smelled delicious.

'She could get *me* a job if she wanted to,' Aunt Seraphina

used to say, day-dreaming over a Rajah's letter of praise. 'But, of course, I have to stay on here, unpaid. I could never leave my dear mother; she needs me. Rosa has all the luck.'

Now, returning, I saw that she no longer envied Aunt Rosa. For Aunt Rosa had been retired for many years, and the glories of that time had faded. Life had equalized their fortunes. It troubled me, as the days went on, that I began to be bored, impatient, with Aunt Seraphina, who had filled my childhood with fascination. I wanted to see her now, as I had seen her then, with a child's non-judging eye. Then she had held the key; now, I saw, with sorrow and loss, that there was no door in which to fit it. We had both changed, the difference in our ages had narrowed. She had regressed; I had grown up.

I began to feel this after the first week. Max did not telephone again, and I fell into the household routine without effort. Why were people who led ordered lives so disturbing? The aunts and Gibby moved from room to room, and yet these rooms were never empty when they left them. The large furniture, the heavy-patterned carpets, the family portraits, waited for their return. It was the same upstairs. The long-dead Braithwaites could not let life alone; they hung on to it, they occupied space with the living, so that the past stirred gently everywhere.

As I wandered about the house, reaffirming my childhood by a touch here and a touch there, in and out of doors that still opened on to 'Uncle Bertie's den', 'Dada's study', 'Aunt Sue's room', 'your mother's bedroom': or ran upstairs to check the right time on my grandmother's little French silver-gilt clock that kept its own hold on the present in her unaltered, shrouded room, I began to realize just what my news must have meant to them all. The letter that had begun the great change.

.   .   .   .   .

It must have arrived at breakfast-time. My grandmother would have smiled, passing it to Aunt Rosa to read aloud, for her own sight was failing. How pleased they would have been to hear from me, safe in the country, away from V2s and buzz-bombs, still at school. I had failed my university examinations, and was trying to make up my mind what career to take up. The school had been evacuated to Hertfordshire and had taken over a farmhouse and several other houses in the village, so that life was rather more lax than the aunts suspected. We had a great deal of freedom, especially the sixth-form girls, and were expected to work on the farm and in the gardens, and 'do our bit'. The atmosphere was a pleasant one of ordered anarchy, and we were curiously immune to world events. To us, harvest-time was the important thing. I did not even bother to listen to the news, for it never occurred to me that we could possibly lose the war. I merely waited for it to be over.

The men employed on the farm were mostly pacifists or army rejects. Max, a pacifist, was employed as gardener and art teacher. At fifteen I followed him about like a puppy, at sixteen I offered to become his mistress, and at nineteen I made up my mind to marry him because he had not taken up my previous offer; and by then the war was nearly over and he would soon leave to follow his own career.

Only this last piece of information was contained in the letter to my grandmother. With the absolute selfishness of first love I demanded her permission to marry. I only asked this, I told her, because I was under age. Otherwise, I threatened, I would surely live with him, and we hoped to raise a large family. 'You'll love Max,' I added, without hope.

Sending it, I had not troubled to imagine their reactions. I only wanted a necessary signature, and then to forget them. Now, in the morning-room where nothing had changed its place since that time, except that the curtains were more faded, a little darned, the cretonne covers worn, I felt, as if I had been there, the subtle shift in the atmosphere, the disturbance. Spoons laid down, rigid faces turned one to another.

'You can't mean it, Rosa. Are you sure the child says that?'

'It's all here, mama. See for – oh, never mind. You read it, Fina.'

Tilting the letter to the light, Aunt Seraphina would have mouthed the words carefully, with little gasping breaths at each comma. She always read aloud as if each printed word held a mortal sting, even fairy stories, and now she was justified; for each word, as she told me afterwards, 'stabbed her to the heart'.

'Who is this man?' would have demanded my grandmother.

'I think he works in the garden. Louie has mentioned him before. And —'

'Works in the *garden*? A *gardener*? I must telephone the head-mistress at once. It's disgraceful. The supervision must have deteriorated. We should never have sent the child there – or never allowed her to go with the school. There have been no bombs in Pagham Green; it was all unnecessary. I blame Jennie Copton for this, Rosa. I lay the blame squarely at her door. She may be your great friend, but —'

'Mama, please don't get excited. We all agreed. You liked the school, and the idea of the farm. It was healthy, you said, and —'

Aunt Seraphina, I am sure, would have broken in here, for she loved a dramatic situation. She would rise to it now, eyes flashing, bosom heaving, making the most of it.

'I never trusted a school that did away with uniforms! No girl gets ideas like this if she is decently clad in a navy-blue tunic. It hides the figure. But you were all against me. Now what happens? Running off with a gardener! What would her mother have said? That child was a sacred trust! We should have had a governess at home.'

'Don't talk such rubbish, Fina! No child has a governess these days! Anyone would think we were made of money! And Jennie's own children are there. Never a word from them —'

'Vipers!'

'Stop quarrelling, both of you. I am going to telephone.' And my grandmother, straight, frail, would have groped for the table-edge, risen, turned to the door, finishing the argument.

As it was a trunk call, there would have been some trepidation and delay. The switchboard was still a manual one and the demand for a trunk call was sometimes beyond the girls' capabilities.

What my grandmother said to Miss Wentworth I was never told. But Miss Wentworth told me that I was summoned home urgently, and was there any truth in the extraordinary news she had heard? My grandmother seemed to think that I was ruined.

'I want to marry Max, or I will be ruined,' I said dramatically.

'Oh? And does Max want to marry you?'

'Of course.'

She was taking it all very calmly. I felt that had I been a real academic, with a scholarship in hand for Oxford, her reactions would have been very different. As it was —

'Will you ask Max to come and see me?' she asked, with something like amusement in her eye. 'And you had better pack. Thank goodness the school play was last week.'

Deflated by her unconcern, her refusal to treat me as a heroine, I flew off down the garden to find Max, who was picking peaches. I shall never forget how he cradled each one in his hand before laying it in a grass-lined basket. The peaches lay there, safe, firm, ready, each with its individual downy bloom.

'Max! My grandmother has telephoned. I'm to go home. There's going to be a row. And Bobby Wentworth wants to see you.'

I was inflamed, sick with excitement and fear. Max slowly laid the last peach in the basket and took hold of my arm. We walked up the garden together, I blundering past gooseberry bushes, not seeing anything but Max, his dark face, the brown arm around my shoulders. Everything else, everyone else, was out of focus.

'Whatever happens,' he said slowly, 'there's no choice. We have to be together now. I'll come up with you.'

'Oh no! Oh no! I'll —'

He had laughed, then; said, 'Don't play-act. This is important.'

After that, time telescoped. Max came up with me, met the family assembled stiffly in the drawing-room. It was like an examination. My grandmother promised to think it over, but said we must wait at least a year, during which time I must live at home with them. We could not think of marrying until Max had found a job. As a concession, we could be formally engaged.

At this I had burst into tears, which brought on an attack of asthma, and the next day, when Max had been sent away, I was in such a fury of resentment, of disappointment, that I forced my grandmother's hand. I told a lie that made me into a cheat and Max into a liar. I don't think she ever forgave me, or Max. And as she died soon after I had taken her signature on that bit of paper to a registry office, she was never to find out. I have wondered, ever since, whether the fact that I could never manage to have a child has been a kind of punishment.

I never told Max why she had changed her mind, and he has never found out either, because we took what little money we had and lived in rooms in Camden Town while he looked for a job. Then we went to Ireland to stay with some friends of his, and I took a job in a bookshop while he painted. For five years I never thought about The Hollies.

All through that time, however, the aunts kept in touch. For years they sent me things : hand-knitted bedjackets from Aunt Rosa ; dresses made by Aunt Seraphina ; an occasional sweater, hand-knitted, for Max. Sometimes Gibby made a cake and, as we ate it, the thought of The Hollies choked me. For it was strange ; the more we travelled – and as restrictions lessened, we were able to spend some time in France, then Spain – the closer I felt to the house by the common. Sometimes it seemed as if it were not Aunt Seraphina writing to me, but as if her disjointed sentences were a communication from another self, part of me that lived as full a life as I was living, but far away, in another place. This is difficult to explain, but it was uncanny, and I didn't like it. I felt as if so much was going on that I ought to know about, and that if I could only merge the two lives, I could become twice the person I was. I suppose that if one lives for long enough in a house the blood-streams mingle. Perhaps it was because every letter ended with the words, 'Don't forget that this is your home.'

Forget! It was impossible to forget. So when we moved back to London, found our flat in Bayswater, and settled down into it, that became a pale substitute for home. I visited the aunts : they bore me no grudge ; they were as strong and as still as growing trees, their roots deep in their own soil. Each visit left me unhappy, unsettled, as if something was unfinished, as if, by that abrupt disruption years ago, I had postponed a showdown. I suppose it was a growing feeling of guilt. Because guilt is a funny thing. It grows in the dark, and each misfortune is a part payment for having got one's own way by cheating. If I could have seen my grandmother before she died and told her that in fact I did not 'have' to get married she might have forgiven me, but I doubt it. I began to feel affronted that she had believed me so readily. Why had she? For she had not questioned it, merely turned her head away in acquiescence. I was reasonably sure she had never told the aunts the reason for her change of mind. She had merely withdrawn into the world of The Hollies, where unpleasant things like passion and unworthy emotions and reality were kept out by the high walls, lapped by the half-tamed acres of the common.

Perhaps, as I have said before, change is the thing we all fear, and that was what I was finding in the house. On the surface the framework was the same, the steel girders inside a strong building that will endure for ever or for a lifetime, which is perhaps the same thing. But if life creates order, order does not create life; and life, as I had come to know it with Max, did not exist at The Hollies. Let me be more precise. I had become accustomed to living in the present, with the future strong and beckoning. This was unavoidable, living as we did in the middle of other people's talents, as if in a perpetual spring. The summer we seldom saw, for the students to whom Max devoted his life moved on as soon as their talents passed the budding stage. We were lost in a grove of half-grown young things. Autumn was a long way off unless we contained it within ourselves, and it was to avoid the inevitable winter that I had come back here.

What was 'here'?

For me, the beginnings. Security. A sense of absolute identity. The past, with its lack of challenge. Who had said that if you take one huge leap in life it exhausts you and you can never take another? It was true. My jump had been too big, taken too soon. I had left one world before I had fully explored it, and this was the pull.

It was a relief to tell myself this, and it heightened my

perception. I noticed little things. Gibby went marketing once a week, back to Parrot Lane where she had once lived, and where food was cheap.

'Why not have it delivered from across the common?' I asked.

'And line that man's nest with gold feathers? No, thank you,' Gibby replied, hauling her heavy basket on to the kitchen table and unloading bruised fruit and mauled-looking vegetables. 'I got all this lot for two shillings. They charge you twice as much over the common.'

'But your bus fares add up to the same price, Gibby!'

She set her lips obstinately.

'That's my concern,' she said. 'I get a cup of tea with one of my neighbours. It's nice to have a chat. It's a day out for me.'

I noticed, too, that the three of them ate very little. A small shepherd's-pie, with cabbage, would be served rather splendidly from Rockingham dishes. Afternoon tea was always spread on a lace cloth, with a silver tray and teapot and milk-jug. But the butter was thinly spread, and unless the jam was home-made, we went without.

I looked about me, too. The velvet curtains needed cleaning; the net ones from Aunt Seraphina's bedroom disintegrated in the wash, and one whole evening was given over to an anxious discussion about replacing them.

'We could use the ones from mama's room,' said Aunt Rosa.

'They're just as bad. The sales will be on soon. I'll see what I can get.'

'Aunt Seraphina,' I said, 'as I'm staying here, I must give you something for keeping me. After all —'

I couldn't have said anything more tactless. The mention of money was a vulgarity, and Aunt Rosa flushed up at once. She was easily annoyed. Her voice became even more precise.

'*Pay* us? Whatever next, child? This is your home; we are your own flesh and blood. There's no question of such a thing.'

'But this is a big house to keep up. Everyone finds living difficult today, with costs rising all the time. I do think —'

'Please, Louie, we are not destitute yet, and I trust we never shall be. We are luckier than a lot of people. We have a home.'

'We have always been careful,' Aunt Seraphina added.

This was certainly true. I had never seen any waste in that house. Even orange and lemon rinds were used up, boiled with sugar to make crystallized peel. Bones were boiled for stock, egg-shells thrown in for further nourishment. Stale bread was either soaked for bread puddings or dried in the oven and then crushed for crumbs to coat ham or fish. Fat was rendered down for dripping; sour milk used for scones or for making cream cheese, with chives chopped in and well-peppered. Fruit from the garden was preserved or made into jam; parsley and herbs dried for the winter in muslin bags.

This economy went further than food. String from parcels was carefully wound up; I never remembered my grandmother buying a ball of string, and when Max did so it seemed a terrible extravagance. Butter and lard papers were saved for greasing cake-tins, greaseproof paper from cereal packets was cut into circles and used for steaming puddings. And in the outside lavatory, neatly strung from a nail, were the coloured tissues that had wrapped foreign oranges. Waste, my grandmother said, was vulgar. God wasted nothing, so how could we?

Most people lived like this in wartime, of course, but The Hollies might have been a beleaguered fortress. The poor, my aunts told me, had only themselves to blame, for they were for the most part improvident. They did not bother to mend their children's clothes, they merely tore them up or threw them away when they went into holes. Privately I thought this a good idea, for I grew tired of dresses and skirts being let out and remade and turned and dyed. Aunt Seraphina was always unpicking seams and dipping old stockings in tea or coffee; one summer she even painted a straw hat she had found in the attics. 'If you wait long enough,' she often said, 'everything will come back into fashion.' And of course she was right. I could today walk out in one of her long-waisted dresses of the twenties, dripping with jet bugles, and not look out of place.

I remembered one act of rebellion on my mother's part. She had once wanted new curtains for my nursery and had been told that there was some good linen in one of the chests in the attics which she could dip and make up. Quietly, she had gone out and bought some bright new chintz. After she had made the curtains and hung them up, my aunts and grandmother came into the nursery and looked at them with pursed lips, then went away without saying a word. They did not like anything new being brought into The Hollies.

The next day I measured the window in Aunt Seraphina's room and went out quietly, like my mother, and bought some nylon net. I said it was a present for the house and waited, apprehensively, for the aunts' reaction.

'This stuff attracts the dirt,' said Aunt Seraphina, fingering it delicately. 'Dust flies on to it. I heard a woman on the wireless say so.'

'But it's so easily washed, and you don't need to iron it.'

Aunt Seraphina pursed her lips. 'The modern way is the lazy way,' she said. 'Whatever next! I can't see how young people fill their lives today, with their washing-machines and their drip-dry clothes. It doesn't do for a woman to have too much spare time; she isn't educated for leisure. On that housing estate down there,' she indicated the direction by a turn of her head, 'the women gossip over their fences

33

and let their children run wild. Or else they take jobs in factories. I don't see,' she went on at random, still fingering the wicked modern stuff with guilty pleasure, 'I don't see what good it does a child to hang a door-key round its neck and give it expensive toys at the same time. Something's gone wrong, Louie. I don't know what mama would say.'

'It's very good of the child,' said Aunt Rosa, coming into the room and folding up the paper in which the material had been wrapped. 'This sort of material is a boon to a busy mother. When I think of the work that went into washing and starching and goffering those baby clothes we used to make . . . Do they use this for baby clothes, Louie?'

'Well, the idea's the same – but better stuff, of course. Pure nylon's no good; the skin can't breathe, so it's hot to wear.'

'Hot! It's unhealthy,' cried Aunt Seraphina triumphantly. 'You're asking for skin troubles —'

'Don't be stupid, Fina,' said Aunt Rosa sharply. 'Your trouble is that you can't move with the times. Haven't you seen Louie's underwear hanging up? It's dry in no time, and no ironing.'

'Well,' said Aunt Seraphina, too astonished by her sister's attitude to attack further, 'Well, dear, it's very kind of you. You've done your best, although I still think it might have been wiser to wait for the sales.' And she gathered up the stuff and sailed out of the room.

'Take no notice,' whispered Aunt Rosa. 'She's as pleased as Punch. She's gone off to make them up. She'll start singing in a minute. Always was a funny girl. By the way, this letter came for you.'

She watched me as I opened it. It looked official, being type-written, so it was not from Max. It also had 'to be forwarded if necessary' on the envelope.

'How extraordinary!' I said, as I read it. 'Look at this, Aunt Rosa. What can he want?'

It was from the family solicitor, and he asked to see me at my earliest convenience as he had something of importance to convey to me.

I burst out laughing.

'Something of importance to convey to me. I don't see —'

Inevitably Aunt Rosa said, with authority, 'There's only one way to find out. You must telephone him and make an appointment.'

FOUR

'It's very fortunate, dear, that young Mr Bradshaw's office is in Baker Street,' said Aunt Seraphina, a day or two later. 'I will come up with you, if you don't object. While you are having your interview I shall stroll through Regent's Park.'

I was surprised, for she seldom went out, but supposed that she was curious about my business with the solicitor and wanted to know all about it before Aunt Rosa. These small rivalries were part of the sad business of growing old. So we set off after lunch and caught a train.

'I can't understand,' she said, loudly and clearly, ignoring the few turning heads in our compartment, 'I can't understand what that young man means when he refers to your father's estate. Your father *had* no estate, and he was a comparatively poor man when he died. After all, he had not worked for years, and I understood that his income died with him. Why, if it hadn't been for mama —'

I stopped her, sensing the wormlike inquisitiveness stirring behind the shut-in, shut-off faces of our fellow-passengers. Also, growing ever since I had arrived at The Hollies was this inexplicable guilty feeling of partisanship for my dead father whom I had scarcely known. How had he fitted into that female world? He would have had no chance at all, for he was a man, a sick one at that, and not a Braithwaite. *Requiescat*. And yet, perhaps he had rested long enough? By what right did the living forget the dead, drive them underground a second time? The solicitor's letter, which had only roused a mild sense of inquiry on a first reading, now seemed a reproving signal from some place very far away from this mild September afternoon. I began to feel that perhaps my father still had something to say, and I also felt that my aunt resented it.

As the train drew into Victoria, she said, 'Let us go straight to the park and look at the dahlias. You can leave me there and go on to the office. We seem to be early.'

We were early.

'Are you going to do some shopping?' I asked, offering to carry the large rush basket she had on her arm. It was very deep, the sort usually used for vegetables. To my surprise she kept tight hold of it and shook her head.

'Shopping? Not exactly. Ah, here's our bus.'

She nipped quickly up the stairs, her neat ankles turning on the dangerous curve as lightly as a young girl's. She was full of pleasure, choosing the front seat and looking around her as we churned up Park Lane in a mass of traffic.

'I hear they intend to make this a – what do you call it – a dual highway,' she said. 'Biting into the park with those dreadful machines! All the same,' she added, as taxis hooted impatiently and people tried to dart across the road, 'it's far-sighted, I'll say that for them. Oh, do look! The caryatids. I love them, don't you?'

The stone female figures bearing a balcony on their heads were almost level with our eyes as we drove slowly on. 'I love being on top of a bus. There's so much to see.'

She made her comments all the way along Baker Street, pointing out this shop and that, leaning down excitedly as we passed a curious, dusty window, full of cardboard cut-outs of women, wearing what could only be described as bust-supports. Necklaces of beads and shells hung from un-likely shelves, and printed notices were stuck up against the kind of bathing-caps that make one look as bald as a peeled egg.

'Miss Meredith was apprenticed there,' she said. 'There's nothing she doesn't know about bust-supports. A friend of mama's went to her after her operation, and you couldn't tell that she had only one breast. That was thanks to Miss Meredith. Still, I can't understand why that shop is still going. Young women today go to Marks and Spencer's, don't they? Jews. And a fancy name for everything.' We approached Hanover Gate and she made ready to get off. As we went down the stairs she turned and said, 'Of course, dear, they're not for normal women. Only for big ones, and nursing mothers, and the diseased.' She levelled a quelling glance over her thin, high-bridged nose at the conductress, who was caught giggling, and to my relief we got off without incident.

'*I* have never needed one,' she added thoughtfully, as we crossed the road. 'Being small. My waist was only twenty-one inches when I was a girl, eighteen pulled in. But then the Braithwaites all have beautiful figures.' She glanced at me sideways, added, 'Of course, dear, you're in proportion, but large-boned like your father.'

Ahead of us the thick pewter-coloured water of the lake gleamed sluggishly, and the sun was reflected from the surface rather than drawn down into it. We went between great beds of geraniums edged with salvia and a pinkish-grey plant that looked like a disease. If creeping alopecia were a plant, then this was it. A tall man with dark hair streaked with grey was feeding half a dozen Chinese geese. They took the chunks of bread from his fingers with strong, uncompromising bites: snakes with beaks. He fed them gravely, like an equal, and he reminded me of Max.

'No nonsense about them,' said my aunt approvingly. 'They know what they want; see how firmly their feet are planted on that path. Sensible birds.' She watched them for a moment and then said, softly, like a conspirator, into my ear, 'Just stay here and watch them, dear. Delightful, quite an education. I must see about those pink geraniums. I don't think we have any quite that charming shade at home.'

Astonished, I turned to see where she was going. She

went to the geraniums and bent over them, examining them closely. A park-keeper appeared and stood by her side. They exchanged a word or two, and then she bade him a brisk good afternoon, and beckoned to me.

'Let's go across the bridge and look at those wonderful dahlias.' So we turned, walking comfortably together in the soft air. The dahlias were magnificent; they blazed at us across the water, their colours shading from white to deepest purple. For some reason I felt completely happy; there was a spaciousness about the afternoon. It was like strolling in a well-cared-for estate. The great willows tickling the water absorbed the sun, so that their leaves gleamed with a liquid green. It was one of those autumn days when the sunlight seemed to mellow everything it touched, enriching the grass, which became greener, and the earth, too, black and sleek. Here there were no extremes, and I was glad that we had not settled in Provence as Max had once wanted to some years ago. The scorched earth, the unremitting sun, the ceaseless noise of those cicadas, demanded something of me I was not prepared to give. As we walked over the bridge, still bordered by its long boxes of trailing flowers, a swan broke the surface of the water as it planed down upon it, leaving a wake like scattered mercury.

'Too many people,' said my aunt. 'I expect the sun brings them out, like wasps.'

She was looking unkindly at the old people dozing on the seats by the hedge, and I was surprised by her fretful tone. Her eyes were restless, as bright as the bird's whose feathers made the hat she wore. A cousin in the country had shot a brace of partridge and sent it to the aunts, so each bird had served a double purpose. We walked lingeringly past the dahlias, peering about for their labels. *Arctic Snow, En Deuil, Rosanna's Blush* . . . Aunt Seraphina sparkled into pleasure once more.

'Oh, do look, Louie. *Mrs Dale*. Hm. Hardly the colour for

her, I'd have thought.' The blooms were large, flaunting, a flaring purplish red. 'More like the *Folies Bergère*. Or *Cancan*. Now there's a marvellous name for a dahlia, or a rose. I should call a black rose – *if* they ever produce one – *Cancan*.' She sighed, 'I should like to go down to posterity by raising a rose called *Cancan*. But, alas, my fingers are not green enough, nor my purse long enough.'

Aunt Seraphina certainly had green fingers. She was a dedicated gardener, and it was said she took after her father in that respect. At The Hollies she had her own greenhouse, full of pots of all sizes, filled carefully with specially sifted earth and compost and peat, enriched by pinches of bonemeal at the right season. It was due to her that the house was never without flowers. We never knew what we were going to find, or where. One year, I remember, quite soon after my mother's death, she went in for trailing, variegated ivy and transcandentia that grew up the dining-room walls on trellis and attracted beetles and spiders and small red flies that dropped into the soup. Her petunias lasted longer than any others I knew. Well into November they were still blooming, long and leggy, against the glass greenhouse walls long after she had taken them out of the hall and the dining-room, where they would be replaced by great urns of yellow pincushion chrysanthemums and flaring dahlias, or bunches of cherry-coloured dwarf michaelmas daisies. She went in for indoor exotics whose names I could never remember, although I never liked the smooth, showy leaves, all blotches or stripes.

I was moved to ask her now how she managed to raise so many plants in the garden at home with so little money to spare.

'I take cuttings, dear,' she said vaguely. 'And of course I collect seeds. Never waste seeds. I shake the heads of the dead flowers into glass tubes and put them in your grandfather's pipe-rack, labelled, so that I know where I am. You must have seen me doing them, silly child.' She looked round restlessly again. 'They've forgotten to take cuttings here. It will be too late when the frosts begin.'

We had crossed the Inner Circle and were round by the tea-house. On to the thick hedge with the door set deep in it. I began to be anxious about the time, but before I could suggest turning back, my aunt spoke.

'Do you remember coming here to see *A Midsummer Night's Dream*?' I nodded.

'We hired a car and drove all the way here and back again. You talked about the fairies. Oh, you loved it.'

Had I? I couldn't be sure. All I could remember was the unnatural green of the bushes behind the grassy stage, and Puck bursting out of a tree to laugh at Bottom with the ass's head. I had been very cold, and an uncle I hadn't seen again had given me a sip of brandy from a silver flask and wrapped me in a blanket.

'You said the fairies were blue with cold, but I told you it was phosphorescence. What a queer child you were!'

But I was thinking what a queer thing memory is. Like a roulette wheel spinning, and the number at which it comes to rest scarcely ever coincides with the one on which you have staked your money. Obviously this time Aunt Seraphina had put hers on red seven. Mine remained, losingly, on black ten. She spoke with resignation, and I could feel her thinking that if *she* had been that child, taken by night to see a play in a park, with fairies and dukes and lovers wandering between green bushes, how she would have *responded*! It was all in her sigh: her lost opportunities for adventure, for love, for self-expression. She was more of a child than I had ever been, and I loved her again for her wild and illogical longings, her aching desire for drama. No physical draw-back like cold or a feared asthma attack could ever come between her and the big romantic moment. It occurred to me with something of a shock, for I had not for years really thought about her, that my aunt had never experienced anything in the flesh. It was all in retrospect, or in the future, or vicarious. But she attracted drama; wherever she was, tension grew up, a dramatic situation was gradually formed. Look at Bruno, for instance; for years an impossible attachment, dismissed by the family because he was 'unsuitable', being married and connected with the theatre. That 'Uncle' with the brandy flask might well have been Bruno, for I had never seen him again. . . . But it was getting late, and I was restless.

'Aunt Seraphina, I think —'

Neither of us wore a watch. We seemed to be allergic to them. Time dashed forward or stopped altogether when strapped to our wrists.

'Are you anxious about your goldmine in the Yukon? My poor child, your father's shares were always countable in postage stamps.'

But her heart was not in teasing me; she was looking around in what I can only describe as a furtive manner. We had crossed the broad path which led to the fountain with mermen and mermaids and shells and were now in a quieter, more isolated part. Her step quickened; she seemed to know the park very well, and it surprised me. People lay back in deck-chairs, their eyes closed, soaking up the vanishing summer. An old man fed sparrows; they were all over him, cloaking his shoulders, edging his worn coat like braid. I looked round to point this out to my aunt, but she was away by a flower border, breaking off geranium shoots with what even I recognized as practised, expert speed. These were rapidly transferred to her bag, and tucked away beneath a copy of *The Times*. She returned, smiling.

'So pretty, with those coloured leaves. I needed some,' she said calmly. 'Now let us see what they have in the Japanese garden.'

'Aunt Seraphina, you can't! You'll be had up! Suppose everybody just took —'

'Hush, child. *Everybody* is not *me*. I understand flowers. They were simply begging to be propagated. There is no crime in simply taking a few shoots to propagate in one's own garden. Think of the next frost: it would be too late. I cannot bear waste, and I told an officious keeper, so, once.'

'You were *caught*?'

'Caught? Come, come. I was *observed*, yes, and given a sharp warning. But I made him understand my views. I explained that it was my money being spent on this park, so I was entitled to a little interest on it. Men are so illogical.'

All I could say was, 'You were lucky not to be fined. I expect they watch suspicious people.'

'I am not a suspicious person, Louise. That keeper I was speaking to at the gates, for instance. I know him. He's an old friend of mine, and I leave his beds alone.' Aunt Seraphina turned her candid eyes on mine and laughed. Clearly, wickedly, like a child who has scored a point. 'They are too near the road, anyway. It would be a bad example to others.'

'Does Aunt Rosa know about this?'

There was a long pause and I realized that I had acted in a beastly way, like a person with a pin. For there are always persons waiting with pins to explode the lovely balloons so hopefully sent up by the unregarding innocent. I was getting over my priggish shock, and had begun to see things Aunt Seraphina's way, realizing as I did so that the Braithwaite way of life was a kind of anarchy that could scarcely be contained within one house. All the same, I suspected that Aunt Rosa would be far from pleased to know that her sister stood in annual danger of being arrested, hauled up before a magistrate and fined.

At last Aunt Seraphina said, idly scanning the borders,

'Your Aunt Rosa is a very limited woman, my dear. We all have our limitations and our sore spots. Do you know, I really think she would view it in the same light as shoplifting.' She raised her eyebrows and laughed to show how absurd the comparison was. 'I regard this park as *my* park, and I bless the Prince Regent for thinking of it, *if* he did. And as I don't object to giving a friend a cutting here and there from my own garden, why should the Royal Commissioners object to giving me a few? I am perfectly willing to do the same for them, *as* I told the keeper; but I fear he regarded it as bribery. One moment, dear, look at those men! Burning leaves! Such waste; think of the compost. . . . I must just . . .' And she went off to scold them.

She caught me up as we turned into Queen Mary's gardens to admire the late roses, and I thanked God she had not been able to secrete a spade. She was quite recovered; the spat with the men had revived her pleasure and twice she bent down to tweak out a root of some pink spiky flower, a kind of polygonum.

'It's a relation of that white stuff that froths over walls. From the Greek. *Poly* meaning many, and *gonum*, well, roots, I imagine. Many-rooted. It's a good deed to keep it in check or it would swamp the park. Some things beg to be divided.'

As she went over the hump-backed bridge into the Japanese garden, I found myself looking at people as they passed by with sharp intensity. Now I was definitely an accessory after the fact, and it was uncomfortable. I feared a hand on my shoulder, a bland inquiring voice.

But when Aunt Seraphina reappeared, she had a young woman with her who carried a trowel and basket and wore blue jeans.

'So kind of you, my dear. You have a lovely garden here. What a splendid show of fragrant heaths. A very worthwhile job.'

44

They parted on the best of terms and, with a sly, triumphant movement, my aunt lifted a corner of *The Times* to reveal several more roots. 'The rockery will be a picture next year,' she said. 'I never thought of just *asking* before. Of course it's all very hushhush, but there's a natural freemasonry between gardeners.'

With her springing step and straight back she walked like a happy young woman. 'And now for young Mr Bradshaw. Not quite a gentleman, of course, unlike his father; but being in the law makes up for that. I shall meet you at Fortnum's for tea, dear.'

I saw her on to a bus, and wondered whether one ever really knows another human being, especially a close relative, but as I turned into the gloomy door of the block of offices, I knew positively where she was bound. She would go straight to the rest-room, and there water and gloat over her plants in privacy. In the meantime I was a quarter of an hour late for my interview with Bradshaw, Bradshaw & Pertwee.

FIVE

My aunt was right. Young Mr Bradshaw was not quite a gentleman. He was not quite a young man either, but he was not a damaged young man, in the Dickensian sense. He was young, of course, in comparison to his father, who had retired from practice, and whom I had met only once, at about the time I married Max. All the same, he was pleasant enough, if foxy. He had a lawyer's face, entirely uncommitted, if one can use the word in that sense, and why not? He had a small greying moustache, pale blue eyes and the beginnings of a pot belly. When we shook hands, it was like shaking hands with a gibbon, so narrow and boneless did his hand seem. By the way he spoke to his secretary I saw that he was a repressed bully. His office had no climate; here it was always between seasons, the brownish panes of glass turning away the sun as had the pewter-coloured water of the lake, and the only warmth was the neutral central heating.

He was aware that I was late, and emphasized it by a glance at his silent electric clock on the brown mantel-shelf. We talked of nothing for exactly two minutes, and then he bowed his head towards some papers on his desk.

'Did you know that your late father held a few shares in the Sunrise Oil Company?' he asked.

I was astonished. I didn't think my father had any investments worth speaking of. I had had a few dividends from time to time over the years, but — I shook my head.

'We've written to you once or twice before, Mrs . . . er . . . Mrs Yeovil. I take it our letters never . . . er . . . reached you?'

'Have you? No. I mean, well, we've been on the move. We were in Europe for several months last year, and this year we spent quite a time in Dublin. I'm afraid —'

'Quite – so.' He spoke deliberately.

'But haven't you our Bayswater address?'

He bent to a machine on his desk and pressed a switch which buzzed.

'Miss Foot, have we a Bayswater address for Mrs . . . er . . . Yeovil? Please check immediately.'

The information came back quickly, and he looked over to me and said, 'Obviously not. We have sent all letters to your aunts.'

'Ah well,' I said, 'they are inclined to be forgetful, you know.'

'Well, in future,' he began; but I could not bear this any longer.

'Mr Bradshaw, why do you want to see me? I can't imagine that —'

He held up a hand, enjoying the moment.

'Do you follow the market? Ah, I thought not. If you did, you would see that oil shares in certain parts of the world – only certain parts, mark you – have had a spectacular rise. Oil is gushing from the deserts, Mrs . . . er . . . Yeovil. Gushing. The deserts are blossoming like the rose. In short, the Sunrise Oil Company have hit it rich.'

I gazed at him, stunned by his flowing periods.

'Oil, Mrs Yeovil, has come into its own. It is a lifeline. Certain companies that we had as good as written off, companies regarded by the Exchange as, let us say, suspect, have become less suspect. In short, you have a nice little nest-egg, and that's always welcome, I take it, if one's name isn't Gulbenkian.'

He gave a dry little laugh, and I asked at once, intrigued, 'How much?'

He waved a gibbon's paw. 'Not a great deal. With interest,

47

up to date' – he glanced down at a slip of paper – 'seven hundred and fifty pounds.'

'But —'

'Let me explain. As your father's legal consultants, we did not sell out at his death. We acted according to his instructions and against our instincts. In his will you inherited all he had, but he made a point of leaving certain shares in our hands, as you were too young to deal with them.' A look of painful embarrassment spread over his greyish, enclosed face. He was going to take me into his confidence, and it was like entering a strong-room. 'Owing to my father's illness the papers were pigeon-holed for many years. When I succeeded him, I found them, and as I am a student of the stock market I made inquiries. With this result. The company in question had transferred the stock to a larger company, and this means that you benefit. Now, do you wish to have the money, or will you allow us to re-invest it for you?'

I have a block where money is concerned. Never having had any, I have never tried to acquire any. Living, as Max and I had done, on the barest margin, the fact that one could juggle with money had escaped me. Money, when one had it, was to use. And we could certainly use that seven hundred and fifty pounds. We? At the moment there was no 'we'. I suppose I would have to have thought of getting a job, of paying my aunts something. They could not have gone on keeping me. I did not like young Mr Bradshaw for reminding me of these matters. When things are in flux, any positive solution is hateful. I tried to think constructively.

'What are the shares doing now?' I asked, with the air of one who is on the ball, however belatedly.

'Rising. Rising,' said young Mr Bradshaw, with a triumphant twitch of the jaw. 'Do I take it you would like to leave the money where it is, or would you care to play the market?'

'Play the market! Good heavens, no. This isn't a fortune, Mr Bradshaw. Let's leave it where it is at the moment. May I have a hundred pounds perhaps? Then I can forget the rest for the moment.'

My mind ran on warm vests for Max; a new sports jacket. Re-cover the divan. A winter coat. Presents for the aunts and Gibby. Seven hundred and fifty pounds seemed a great deal of money to me. I had never possessed so much at one time. Oddly enough, it made me uncomfortable.

Mr Bradshaw looked a little disappointed. He wanted to prove his skill, I could see that; so I asked him what he would advise.

'Spread the load. Say a couple of hundred in these new Unit Trusts, if you don't want to gamble. Leave the rest where it is. Do you like to gamble, Mrs Yeovil?'

He had my name without hesitation at last and I was duly grateful.

'I don't think I'm interested in gambling, at least not with money,' I said. 'There's so much else, isn't there?'

His pale eyes creased with an effort at amusement.

'Ha, yes. Yes. I do see. Ha, yes indeed. So much else – that's very good. Well, in the meanwhile, then —'

'I'd like a cheque for a hundred pounds.' It sounded brutal.

A hundred pounds. I couldn't believe it. 'And thank you for taking such good care of my affairs, I really am most —'

'There's something else, 'said young Mr Bradshaw. 'I nearly forgot. How remiss of me.'

He opened a brown folder and took out an envelope, handing it to me across the desk with a smile that bristled his moustache and lifted his upper lip; a hare or rabbit on the scent. So many small animals he reminded me of, never a man. As I took the envelope, reading my name on it as it had been before my marriage, I felt a stab of disbelief and a strong urge to hand it straight back.

'Your father left instructions that this letter should be given to you either when you reached the age of thirty, or if the shares amounted to anything substantial, before that date. That only came to light, I'm afraid, when the office was reorganized. However, by your papers I see that we are only a few months out. You have passed your thirtieth birthday? Not by much, I imagine. I know what ladies are about their age.' He looked at me speculatively, as if he had caught me in my underclothes. As I hesitated to take the envelope, he shook it gently at me. 'Your father was an unusual man, Mrs Yeovil. Not eccentric, exactly, but well – unusual. He may have further instructions for you. Quite a far-sighted man, your father. His death so young was a tragedy.'

I scarcely listened. My hands were clammy with the shock of seeing this writing again after so many years. It was curiously like my own, but more elegant, more disciplined. How long since had he died? And why young? One's parents were never young. What could he possibly have to say to that eight-year-old who had watched him cough away that last hot summer? It was like taking up a postcard that had for some reason never been delivered at the right time, and seeing the date from a time out of mind.

Before I slit the envelope I asked for a glass of water. Guiltily, Mr Bradshaw said at once, pushing the buzzer once more, that it was tea-time anyway: he would ask his secretary to bring an extra cup. I shook an Ephedrin from the tube and waited. It was becoming a pointless game seeing through young Mr Bradshaw, and I had no energy to waste. I would need it all to combat the tightening band round my chest. I supposed it was the shock that had brought it on.

Ignoring the curiosity that leapt the space between us, I began to read. First the date.

'June Twenty-first, 1935.

My dearest daughter,

Lou darling, I wonder whether you will ever read this letter? Lawyers are funny animals and old Bradshaw may well be dead or forget. In any case, I doubt whether these shares will ever come up, for I am not a man of business. I hope they do, and I hope, too, that they will give you a little money of your own which you will enjoy spending. If they don't, try not to condemn me, because if you are now thirty, your opinions will be formed, although I trust not hardened, for one must try to keep fluid.

Are you married, I wonder? Have you children? I hope so, for you have given me great joy, and it is hard to know that I will die before knowing what kind of life you will make for —'

A cup of tea was put beside me, with sugar in a tiny Cellophane bag I could not open, so I drank it without, swallowing the tablet.

'There's nothing here about re-investing,' I said. 'It's just a gift, my father says. Sorry about this. I'll be all right in a moment.' I put the letter in my handbag. It was not the kind of thing to read under such alarmed scrutiny.

'Really, I'd no idea you suffered from these attacks. The shock, of course. Your father had a weak chest. I remember seeing him when I was a boy, most distressing. Can I —'

'Don't worry,' I said painfully. 'You can't die of it.' Already it was passing off; it was only slight, and the ache across the chest, the racing of the heart, told me it was on the way out. 'You've no more secret documents to wait until I'm forty?' I asked, trying to lighten the atmosphere. I knew it was alarming for people to watch, and felt guilty at causing him distress in his own office.

He responded at once, enormous relief humanizing him.

'Drink your tea,' he said, almost kindly, 'Or would you prefer another cup? That's nearly cold.'

I explained that I was meeting my aunt for tea, and got up to go.

He wrote out the lovely cheque and I put it away safely.

'My regards to the three ladies,' he said. 'I wish their shares could rocket, too. Some time I must have a talk with Miss Rosa – I mean, Mrs Statham – I can't think of her as a widow, isn't it strange? She's always the eldest of the Miss Braithwaites to me.'

There was something in his manner that made me think about the shabby curtains, the unremitting economy of the household.

'Mr Bradshaw,' I said, standing by his desk, 'I don't want to probe, and I know you must be discreet. But I think things are perhaps . . . well, difficult for my aunts. People on fixed incomes must find it difficult today. Perhaps a transfer of shares, or —'

To my surprise his affability vanished. He looked at me stiffly, as if weighing up my right to ask such a thing, and my real reason for so doing. He must know that I was closer than anyone else to my aunts and perhaps suspected me of entertaining 'expectations'. He made me feel guilty of a vulgarity.

'Aunt Cissie is all right, I know that,' I plunged on. 'But the other two . . . Well, there they are, keeping up a big house, and they're getting on. Naturally, I'm concerned for them —'

'Naturally,' he repeated, dryly.

I could have sprung on him and dipped his head in the inkpot, but I held my ground, gazing at him steadily.

'I cannot divulge my clients' business, as you know, Mrs Yeovil. I would not have dreamed of telling your aunts of *your* good fortune. But, yes, I do agree, that some review of the position is due.'

'Then you'll be in touch with Aunt Rosa? Naturally I

won't say a word. She doesn't care to discuss financial matters with me.'

'A lady of the old school,' he said, with a reverential bow. He shot out his hand with a sudden jauntiness, swivelling his plump little body round as if my hand were a screw he had difficulty in turning, then let me go abruptly and propelled me through the door. I had wasted enough of his valuable time.

On the bus to Piccadilly I resisted the temptation to look again at my father's letter. It was unreal, faintly sinister, this signal from the past, and yet, recalling my feeling on the train coming up, was it so unexpected? In my experience life moved in a series of unconnected jerks, which eventually formed a pattern. And it would be something to read, secretly, in bed.

As for the money, that was too true to be good. All I had to spend it on at this moment was Aunt Seraphina, and it would give me a sad pleasure to watch her innocent greed as she lapped up rum baba and *marrons glacés* in the expensive, carpeted Aladdin's cave that was Fortnum's to her.

SIX

I PLEADED TIREDNESS and went off to bed early that night.
This suited the aunts, as they liked to have everything locked
up, the house impregnable, before ten, a practice which
irked me, as I was used to late hours.

'Don't read too long and try your eyes, dear,' said Aunt
Rosa. To her, reading was a faintly suspect occupation,
especially in a woman. She had done her best to stamp out
this bad habit in childhood, and had only succeeded in
making me both obsessive and guilt-ridden about it. I
refused to make any concessions, and although I did not
intend to open it, took up a book I had borrowed from the
study, one of a set of Buffon. Carrying it, I crossed the room
to kiss them good night.

They both laid down their work: Aunt Rosa her darning
(she was looking over her bedsocks for the coming cold
weather), and Aunt Seraphina her embroidery. It pleased
them never to be idle, to show themselves busy.

'Good night, my dear girl,' said Aunt Seraphina, some-
what surprisingly, and kissed me strongly. 'You're wise to
go to bed early, with all this excitement. It's been enough
for one day. I *have* enjoyed myself.'

'More than enough, I'd say,' added Aunt Rosa, clicking
her teeth. It was all beyond her, she admitted as much, but
she was glad for me. 'Especially now.' She spoke with
emphasis, but could not be persuaded to say anything further, although she looked significant enough, nodding with
closed lips. We had talked the subject over from all angles.
I had described young Mr Bradshaw, retailed what he had
said to me and what I had said to him, produced the cheque
and explained about the shares. I had not spoken more than

passingly of my father's letter, neither had I offered to produce it. They approved of the cheque, to them it represented security without ostentation, but the idea of a letter – no, that was a little, well, *overdone*.

Once in bed, I settled back against the pillows and let go. The tiredness ran down my body and out of my toes. It was wonderful. After a few moments I opened my eyes and took up the thin pages of the letter.

'Lou darling, I wonder whether you will ever read this letter? Lawyers are funny animals and . . .'

I scanned the rest of the page. This I had read. On the next page the writing was different, the ink another colour. Perhaps he had written it in the garden, for a small insect was crushed above the second word of the first paragraph. Lying there under covers to take advantage of the sun, writing this in an idle moment, to entice the future towards him. I was right, for the letter went on:

'A child's teeth are set on edge by the grapes of his father's growing, or so they say, but I have given you few grapes. I can only pass on to you the thoughts I've had whilst lying here in this garden under the watchful attention of your aunts. I've been thinking about the relationship between men and women. One is forced into such thoughts here, I being the only man, and probably a dying one at that. Perhaps, by the time you read this, a different kind of partnership will have evolved. I could wish for a new kind of feminine independence, not, God help us, the suffragette kind. Nor the Braithwaite kind. But the kind that makes for inter-dependence in marriage: two human beings loving one another and not desiring to dominate or possess. I expect by this time you have read, or seen *Candida*. She is my most unfavourite female, and Shaw certainly portrayed a few horrors.

'There must be less violence between men and women. This may sound strange, coming to you from me, but there is so much at the present time. This house has seen a great deal of it, under the surface of course . . . just a moment, your Mother is bringing me a cup of tea, bless her. There is no violence between *us*, none at all, for I believe she loves me, although I am no use to her. Thank God she will have a home here with you when I'm gone. She is like a small gay bird, now she's running over the lawn on her thin legs to Seraphina who is cutting gladioli for the house. But life blows cleanly through her. She refuses to acknowledge the shadow, let alone live under it. She lives in the present and does not care to think of tortuous things. She is happy here – what a pull it has, the Braithwaite ambience . . .'

My door opened a crack, and Aunt Rosa's voice said, 'Shall I switch off the light, dear, to save you getting out of bed?'

Scarcely knowing where I was, I at once said, 'Yes, please,' and the light clicked off. I sensed the satisfaction in my aunt's smile as she went off along the corridor to her own room. It is, after all, only human to be pleased when you get your own way.

So I lay in the dark, my hand on the thin, crackling, still unread pages and watched my father in the garden. The back of his neck was very thin, and made him vulnerable.

It was as if a very small film was being run before my closed eyes, about a foot in front of them. I saw my mother run across to Aunt Seraphina, who turned, cutters in hand, an old green straw hat on her head. Then it changed to the kitchen: a child sat at the table cleaning silver with a younger Gibby, still in possession of her own hair; the door opened, my mother came in, her arms full of gladioli spikes, pink and red. She looked windblown and happy.

The film snapped off and the ordinary dark returned. I invented. What had she said? Where had she put the flowers? Had I been sent out to collect the teacup and had I noticed my father writing on a large pad? But the leggy child crossing the garden, now beginning to be shadowed by the creeping evening sun, was my own creation; there was no truth in it. How to nudge memory back? Read some more and trust to a chain reaction, one picture stimulating another?

I groped for a cigarette. Remembered I had hidden them in the painted chamber-pot in the discreet cupboard by the bed. This served most conveniently as ash-tray and hiding-place, and it did not trouble me to realize that in the last week or two I had slipped back into several small childish deceits. Tomorrow I must buy a torch; then I could read in comfort. As I smoked, watching the glow, something else I had quite forgotten jumped into my mind. The candles! Of course. Was it remotely possible that they were still in that secret drawer in the desk. . . ? They had been hidden there to enable me to read in bed, oh, it must be nearly twenty years ago.

I got out of bed, crunching my toes on the cold linoleum, and with a childish sense of trepidation and pleasurable guilt put my hand into the bottom drawer, then on to a sliding piece of wood at the back. My fingers closed with disbelief on two hard sticks. I scratched them. They were wax; it curled up under my nails.

Back in bed, I set them alight, carefully letting wax drip down into the bottom of the chamber, which I set between my knees. Then the candles stood upright and burned, illuminating the tall stork and red roses in that cold china cave. That such a small thing could give one such a sense of triumph! It occurred to me that by the one major act of defiance, that of leaving home, I was absolved from all petty guilt. That action had been too large, too final. It was right outside the Braithwaite code, so they could not touch it. But here was my poor father, conspiring with me, able only to escape by setting down words that might never have been read.

'Has it ever occurred to you, Louise' [I read on] 'that the

Victorian age probably produced more victims than any other? Other ages might be more horrible in their outright oppression, their cruelty . . . but think of those so-called golden years of Victoria: she shrank to a tiny bobbin figure bound in black (I just remember her), shut up in her ludicrous, obsessive grief. She bound the whole nation in crape for fifty years. It was an age to breed eccentricity; it ate up energy, gulped aspirations whole, was made impotent by morality. Freud was thrown up by it, as were Butler, Darwin, Shaw. They were squeezed out of the monstrous complacency of that age like pus from a boil. Men were the reformers, conquerors gulping empires whole, and women were the victims. The very climate of thosey ears ate up their nervous energies.

'Take Seraphina, now. She is full of it; she brims over with nervous fancies; she is, like all the Braithwaite women, full of illusions. Her relationship with the wretched Bruno is one of them, but you probably don't know about that. She is running to waste, and fancies herself the least wasteful of women. In this big, echoing house she has been kept like a prisoner, looking after the children your grandmother has so regularly produced. . . . Yes, a frenetic example of misapplication.

'You are too young to know the atmosphere of this house. It is like living in a minefield; confined energy in tins buried and waiting for the unwary foot. Emotions, activities, all narrowed to a small compass, like a hospital ward or a prison camp. Nothing from the outside seeps in, except, of course, newspapers, but they disregard these. The fierce light of self-regard (without the objective sanity of self-analysis) beats down on them all. I wish I had time to tell you —'

The writing sloped down here and obviously his fountain-pen had run out. There was not much more. A fresh sheet, dated October 15th, 1936. St. Mark's Hospital.

'I have destroyed a good deal of what I wrote to you, and scarcely know what I am putting into this envelope. I hope the shares will one day bring you a surprise. I cannot believe what I write, although by now you know it, even as I write, and you did not cry. Your mother is dead. It is absurd and wicked. A chill, influenza, which is raging just now. I could wish myself less weak and fuller of wisdom and advice. As it is, things must take their course. Only remember, you are only half Braithwaite. There is something of my family in your blood. And if life does not go well for you, think twice before you blame other people. Lying here, in this hospital room, I am sure that the old man's suicide had a far greater effect on the girls than they will ever acknowledge. It may give a clue to their oddness. Don't, for your own sake, be misled by the cultivated exteriors of your aunts. They can smother, they can crush, they can exterminate.

'I am giving this to Sister to post to old Bradshaw. It will be safer with him. By my calculations you might, with luck, have about £400 by your twenty-first birthday, and this letter as my greetings. I have left you a case of small, valueless things back at the house and doubtless Fina will give it to you. They are just mementoes. I have made my will. Should there be no money after all, and you are thirty before this comes into your hands, forgive me. Why thirty? Because you were born when your mother was that age. She had a difficult time. Also because you are in the prime of life and will know which way you are going. Also because it may help you to understand your family. And to encourage you to know that it is never too late to take a new direction. Study your enemies, and cherish your friends.

'I don't think they will bring you to see me again, somehow. Good-bye, my darling, and forgive this self-indulgence.'

The candles, drowning in their wax, smoked nauseatingly. One wick had curled over and I blew it out, pinched it off. The standing birds, the roses, were filmed with smoke. The rest of the room was dark, and it seemed as if all light, all vision had narrowed to that small, stinking cave between my knees. I was extremely cold, and had been crying for some time.

I packed everything away in the cupboard, slid under the

bedclothes, shocked by the disordered tone of the letter, shocked by the word *suicide*. I lay a long time, wide awake, furious that memory should be so patchy, that a child could be in a house and yet not of it. When I eventually fell asleep, I felt in some way mocked.

SEVEN

SOME SOUNDS ARE so strong, so compelling, that they seem to impose on themselves shape and colour. The blackbird's song at dawn therefore penetrated my uneasy sleep in the form of a golden spiral, springing and pulsating in clear airs. I at once wanted to be out in the free morning, away from the thickened atmosphere of my bedroom, which now hid more secrets.

I dressed and went downstairs. The house was absolutely quiet behind its closed doors, alive in sleep, and I went through the drawing-room on the padded strokes of a tall clock in the hall, and out on to the terrace. The lawn was strange with dew where the trees still laid their shadows. To the east the sun was rising out of a red mist. It was like deep country, with no one astir, a rediscovery, to be up so early, so alone, as if the world were empty.

The garden was as secret and as surprising as in my childhood; it had not shrunk, down the perspective of years. On the contrary, it seemed to have extended itself as I stood on the paved terrace, looking down into it at grass and shrubs and flower-beds, and beyond them to the neglected orchard. Then I stepped down on to the shining grass and walked across it, leaving footprints, and made for the cobwebby shrubbery which was pearled as if for a gala.

Behind the shrubberies were the rotting garden sheds, my aunt's greenhouse, and what used to be the kitchen garden, with the raspberry canes, the cordoned peaches, nectarines and pear trees.

Years ago, when the Braithwaite children were small, they had been told to keep to the odd, unhusbanded parts of the garden, to the narrow orchard, the shrubberies. The gardener had told them not to rootle about in his sheds spoiling his geranium cuttings and tulip and daffodil bulbs, not to trample on the dahlia tubers or gladioli corms that lay snug and dry in brown sacking among the bundles of raffia and carefully oiled garden tools. So they had made secret hideaways and tree houses, which I had found in my lonely explorations. I liked to think of the Braithwaite children, at high summer, silent in apple trees, pinafored among the leaves and fruit, spying out the limits of their father's property, watching the neighbours and the people on the common. Gibby had told me many a story about them. How, one day, Bertie, the eldest, had walked all along the wall that bordered the common, so that the door-bell rang all morning with complaints from the owners of the other gardens. My grandmother had chased him as he reappeared, waving a cane and calling to him to come down. But he had not come down. He had jumped for the chestnut tree, then for the swing, missed his hold and fallen. Throwing the cane away, grandmother came running, and gathered him up without a tear, Gibby said, while his blood soaked into her white lawn blouse. . . .

'He didn't die, though?' I would ask at this point, ready to cry.

'Die! Bertie was too tough for that. No, he had a dozen stitches in his head, and a good beating from his father when he was well enough.' Gibby would shake her head in admiration. 'Always up to some devilment, that boy. Always running away, and being brought back.'

He would have run through the gate on to the common, to play with boys of his own age: forbidden children. So, curiously, there I made my way, along overgrown paths bordered with low box hedges. It was evident that no one ever came here now. It had a rank feeling, deep in the shade of tall lime trees that bordered the path outside on the common. The gate itself was almost hidden under the finest blackberry bush I had ever seen; the berries were twice as big and twice as black as the ones on the common. I pulled myself up on the wall beside it, and began to pick off berries, looking idly up the garden and over the common. I was completely hidden from the house, even from the lawn. So why this feeling of being watched? It must have been because I was thinking about the children, I told myself. They had watched everybody: the entwined couples making for the bushes, the great bounding dogs, the shouting boys. Then, turning their sharp eyes from the forbidden territory, they would have watched the polite diversions of their Edwardian parents and neighbours: the croquet and the clock golf, the languid badminton, the parties on the terrace.

They had probably locked the gate for good after some escapade of Bertie's. I looked up, my mouth full of black-berries, and saw, over among the bushes on the common, on a path that ran to one of the broad walks, a man watching me. A very stiff, tall man; and he was immobile and as potent as a totem pole. He was too far away for me to see any details, but as I moved on the wall he lifted his stick and shook it at me, then stared once more.

Unnerved, astonished, I slipped down from the wall and peered through an opening near the gate where the bricks had broken off. He watched for another full minute, then slowly turned and went off beyond a clump of trees, with a gait like a totem pole walking. His presence made the common even more deserted, and emphasized my own soli-tude. Surely only a tramp would be up so early? Or he might be an insomniac, and think I was a burglar.

I badly wanted a cup of tea, and the absolute quietness, apart from the bird-song, which had circled in on the garden from the scattered trees far away, began to disturb me. The thought drifted into my mind of my father walking here, years ago. Under those immense lilac bushes perhaps he had lain in his long chair, covered with rugs, writing to me. I would never know the exact circumstance, nor see him, nor hear his voice. Yet Dunne spoke of serial time, as if scenes could be recorded and run back as if on tape. But in my moment of time, the *now* of this too-bright start to an autumn day – it was sure to rain later – I was nearly the age he had been, busy dying under the aunts' vigilant eyes. To run back time would be to reduce myself to an eight-year-old, so that he would be even further beyond my reach. At least now I had a certain adult perception.

What sort of man, then? He walked like a stranger through my mind, his character traced by his letter, which I could not forget. A man full of half-expressed ideas, a man without a platform. I saw clearly his strong talker's face, the story-teller's sly and lively eye and long, straight mouth. The aunts used often to exclaim, 'Isn't that child the image of Gordon!' looking particularly at my thick, vigorous hair which sprang, curling, from the temples. I never saw the likeness myself, for my father was a handsome man. The leonine head was sadly betrayed by the sag of his body, his shoulders bowed with coughing. He had the muted air of a semi-invalid, as if he no longer counted and knew it. He was dwarfed, in fact, and in my esteem, by the tall and vigorous women of my mother's family, who filled the days with their women's business and tidied him away under his covers; feeding him as one would a household pet, but one which had no entertaining tricks. If he ever had any hope, the Braithwaites had quickly extinguished it. It was a pity, grandmother had said one day within my hearing, that Mary had ever married him: I had gone away to cry about it, and for a week had been especially nice to my father, sharing his shame. Then I forgot him, as I forgot my tortoise while it was hibernating. It was natural for a man to count for nothing at The Hollies. Men brought mess and trouble and women tidied up and sighed. One learnt bite by bite with one's bread and butter that the aunts were never wrong.

Now he had neatly upset those ideas. Peacefully lying there, he had been hating them all, summing them up, writing about them. I reached the rose arbour, which was now a ruin, with the rustic arches down, and the unpruned ramblers lying over the stone seat where we had sat together to read. He refused to read fairy stories to me, choosing instead Celtic hero-tales: Rhiannon and Pwyll; Bran, son of Llyr; Branwen sitting in Harlech castle; Cuchulain and Finn MacCool; Arthur and Merlin and Lancelot . . . these were the names that ran like comets through the summer afternoons. I had a strong stomach for bloodshed.

That violence, it now occurred to me, had carried through to his letter. Although there was a current of pity in it, as if he had at last come to terms with the Braithwaites and, understanding them, could be free. He would have got on well with Max. And yet I resented his words: the aunts loved me, they would not harm me. How dare he *warn* me, and what did he mean about suicide? I had heard nothing about it. And where had grandfather done it? And how? *Why?*

I started to run back to the house, for the confusion in my mind, and perhaps the sharp dewy air, made me cough. The hateful constriction began, and I knew I must get up to my room to the life-saving Ephedrin.

By the time I reached the house I was creeping along, red-faced with what seemed a gigantic effort, and I clung to the kitchen door, panting harshly. Someone was in there. It was Gibby. She turned, a match in her hand ready to light the gas under a kettle, and came to me at once with a chair.

'Sit down, lovey,' she said. 'Where are your tablets?'

I gestured, upstairs.

This was the safest room in the house, and I knew it by heart. Nothing had changed in Gibby's kitchen. The long green sausage filled with sawdust still kept out the draughts from the back door; the wallpaper was the same peculiar shiny buff and the linoleum honey-brown, well polished, with two rugs. This was the only change; sisal striped rugs instead of rag. They must have worn out at last.

The Ideal boiler, its front open, glowed red; the clothes airer was pulled up high to the ceiling, stockings dangling from it. Brass warming-pans and silver meat-covers hung from the walls. The big deal table under the window faced the little brown hide sofa with its patchwork cushions and its magazines that ended here when the family had finished with them. Gibby had claimed the sofa when it was thrown out of Aunt Sue's room years ago, saying that it was just the thing for her to put her feet up on while she waited for a cake to rise. Everything was ordered and peaceful. The scrubbed pine dresser bore the every-day blue-and-white plates, while a matching soup tureen held oddments like buttons and pencils and loops of string and an occasional lemon straying from the larder in the scullery next door. There was a smell of space and scrubbed wood, and coke. And because the autumn was coming, a heavy green serge curtain hung on brass rings over the back door, through which I had recently pushed my way.

Gibby must have run, old as she was, for she was back before the kettle boiled, shaking two tablets into my hand, handing me a glass of water.

She left me alone then, to set out cups and saucers, prepare the small Japanese trays for the aunts' tea. I was in my private hell of blackness and fear of death. I was even beyond telling myself to relax and breathe from the stomach, and clutched at the underside of the wooden chair with clammy hands. At last I was able to look up, while Gibby gently massaged my neck and back, easing my shoulders down from their tense hunching. I coughed, experimentally, and the worst was over. Sippets of air – absurd to think of them like that, with so much of it about – began to push their way into the thousands of tiny cells that had been crushed by that devilish iron hand. Detachedly, I could almost see them revive.

'Drink this,' said Gibby. 'I've given them theirs. A nice cup of tea will soon put you right.' She knelt to take off my shoes, and felt my feet. 'Tch, tch, you're wet through. What have you been up to, out so early?'

But she was only talking to reassure us both; she didn't expect a reply. Soon, apart from the rapid beating of my heart and the sore, stretched feeling in my chest, I was able to move across to the little hide sofa.

'That's it,' said Gibby. 'Put your feet up.' And she wrapped them in an old woolly cardigan hanging behind the door. She wiped my sweaty face with warm water and a clean towel, and handed me a cup of tea. Only then, I saw, did she drink hers, sitting at the end of the sofa as she used to do years ago when I was small.

The tea was hot, and the best thing I had ever tasted.

'I've been much better lately,' I managed to grind out, annoyed. 'I can't understand why —'

'Well, we don't live on the equator,' said Gibby, cryptically. 'It's a nippy old morning to go running around the garden with nothing on.'

Gibby's face was almost square, her jaw thrust forward because she refused to wear her bottom set of teeth unless visitors were expected. She seldom laughed outright, and had caught the aunts' brickbat humour. I had heard her say in shops, 'Oh yes, I'll have a dozen of *those*,' if she knew the price was beyond her. I was grateful to her now for putting this attack down to wet feet. Max would have analysed the situation beyond bearing.

To keep her with me, and to start finding out things that had been kept from me, I asked, as she rose to pour me another cup of tea, 'Gibby, tell me again, how long have you been with the family? Long before I was born, surely?'

67

She shut her eyes and sat back, cradling her cup in her hands, her little legs barely touching the ground. In her blue print dress and apron, the immaculate black wig, she looked like a doll in a doll's house.

'Now, let's see. I came to help Mrs Perkins as was cook; snip of a kid I was then. Your grandma had four staff living in, and that'd be well before the Great War. Jim and me now, we came in every day like. Jim cleaned the shoes and chopped wood – oh, a proper terror, Jim was! Then he and Master Bertie ran off and joined up, and Jim got killed and the mistress said it was all Master Bertie's fault for encouraging him. I was sweet on young Jim, I don't mind tellin' you, but all we could do was wave 'em good-bye.' She raised a hand absently, let it drop. 'I've hated the sound of men marching ever since; turns me up. They'd give 'em good leather on their feet for a war, right enough, but let 'em rot in peacetime —'

I interrupted, 'Gibby, what about my grandfather? Was he in the war, too?'

She looked at me, half in, half out of that far time; then she said, surprised, 'Bless you, no, dearie. He was dead long before the Kaiser started his tricks. Well, say a year, I don't know. Shot himself, poor gentleman —' She stopped, clapped a hand over her mouth, horrified.

'It's all right, Gibby. I knew. I'd just like to know why.'

'You knew? You can't know. Who told you? Not my two ladies, I'll lay!'

I hesitated. 'My father told me.'

She jumped off the sofa angrily, snatching my cup from me. 'Now don't you tell me lies, Miss Lou! You weren't more than a child when he died, and I'm sure *he* wasn't told – unless your mother . . .'

'She must have told him. Anyway, it's all in a letter.'

'All in a letter! That'd make pretty reading. The idea! Miss Seraphina would kill him if —'

'He's dead, so she can't.'

'Anyway, I must get the breakfast, else they'll be down and nothing ready. If I was you, Miss Lou, I'd go up and get back into bed and let Gibby bring you up a hot-water bottle and something nice on a tray. Now you do that and forget all that old nonsense. They'll notice you're queer: there's nothing they don't see.'

Retreat was the best part; she was right. All the same, at the door I couldn't help turning and saying, 'But Gibby, you're one of the family, too. It isn't fair that no one should tell me these things. I'm not a child. Let's have a talk about it, eh?'

'I'm one of the family, right enough,' returned Gibby, with Aunt Cissie's hoarse little laugh. Then, with Aunt Cissie's bitterness, she added, '*And* I've never left it, like some I know. Off you go, now. But I'm promising nothing, mind.'

That was good enough for me. I had always been able to get round Gibby.

EIGHT

LUCKILY IT WAS Aunt Rosa's afternoon for visiting Miss Protheroe in Chestnut Crescent, so she and Aunt Seraphina had an early lunch before she went off. They let me sleep on, having agreed that the early morning air was most treacherous and that there was nothing like a nice rest. Aunt Seraphina looked in to say that she was getting grandfather's study ready for Aunt Cissie, who was arriving the following afternoon. I could help Gibby clean the silver and brass if I wanted to. There was a fire in the kitchen, but I wasn't to tire myself.

I felt fine as I came downstairs. So little happened at The Hollies that the unburying of a family secret promised high drama. How much Gibby would tell me I couldn't guess, for she had had time to think it over and, with the contrariness of old age and her loyalty to the aunts, might very well say nothing at all.

Gibby had the things all ready on the kitchen table, set out on newspapers. Not for her the new short cuts to cleaning; there were the saucers ready, the bottle of methylated spirits and the tin of pink cleaning-powder, old toothbrushes, soft brushes and polishing cloths. It had always been a privilege to assist at this ceremony.

She looked grave, as if aware of the solemnity of the occasion, and handed me an old toothbrush like a priest consigning a censer to an altar boy. As in the old days she poured some powder into a saucer and carefully, drop by drop, added methylated spirits until the paste was like a thin cream. She had never allowed me to do this, and I did not attempt to do so now. I took up a fork, and she said, 'Don't scamp it, Miss Lou. Get in between the prongs.' I dipped my

70

toothbrush into the paste and rubbed, up the engraved handle and well into the curly initial B set at the top. Both sides; then I took up another.

Gibby had started on the entrée dishes, using a soft cloth. To my surprise both sets of teeth were in. She could have been a family lawyer sitting there, with bad news of a will.

'No,' she said, after looking over to see whether I was using too much paste, and as if carrying on a conversation only recently broken off, 'I didn't think I'd stay on after poor Jim was killed. We were sweet on one another, Jim and me. But with one and another leaving, I said I'd live in if they wanted, and help with the children. I was that fond of your ma, being one of the youngest. She wasn't one to quarrel, Miss Mary. Not like the rest of 'em. I remember one day stopping Miss Rosa throwin' a doll of Miss Fina's out of the window. And tease! She was a terrible tease. She'd wait on the stairs in the dark, and jump out and nearly frighten the others to death. Miss Seraphina was frightened of the dark, too, especially after what happened.'

I couldn't imagine my placid Aunt Rosa jumping out at anybody, but I merely said, 'I expect it upset grandmother, didn't it?'

'Upset! Poor lady, she took to 'er bed. Nurse day and night, and nobody thought she'd ever have the baby. In bed a month, too, after; wouldn't look at it.'

That must have been Aunt Sue, unless Gibby was getting muddled.

'But she was the favourite, so they all say.'

'Later on she was. Come as a gift, vicar said. Oh, she was pretty, like a little doll, she was, prettiest of the lot. Foreign blood somewhere, see. And the last born. But oh, how your grandma cried! Didn't want her, not one bit.'

The green plastic handle of the toothbrush slowly flicked back and forth as Gibby took over the polishing of the forks. She was off again, in another direction. The past teemed for her, there was so much; she was almost beyond selecting from it.

'Family wanted it hushed up, of course. Only natural that was, coming so soon after that other nasty business on the common. But it told on the poor gentleman's mind. . . .' I could have shaken her. What other nasty business? But it was best to let her run on in her own way, for she had begun to enjoy these old dry bones, buried so long. Her little black eyes gleamed.

'Wait a bit. He'd been excited, terrible excited. Some old flowers or other up there in his greenhouse. So he'd be up early and we'd always be calling him for breakfast. But one day, I called and called, and still he didn't come. So the mistress had hers with the older children, and went up to her sewing-room. Then there was a knock on the door. Gwennie and me were wondering whether to clear the table or not, and she come back to me with a face like paper. "It's a copper," she says. "Well, call the mistress," I told her. "Oh, I daren't," says she. "You go, Fanny." Silly thing she was then, and acted bad afterwards as well.

'So I went upstairs and called the mistress. How that policeman broke it to her, I don't know, but she came out to us in the kitchen and says to Mrs Perkins that there's been an accident and they're bringing the master home now.'

Gibby fell silent, and we worked on in silence. Outside, the long rain slanted down, darkening the day. From here I could see across the paved yard, down into the garden. Where had they found him?

'He was by the gate on to the common. Outside, of course. I watched them carry him up and over the terrace in through the drawing-room. Covered him up, they had, with a blanket. Mrs Perkins had to have her sal volatile, and the mistress had to slap Gwennie because of her hysterics. Accident, the family said, and accident was on his death certificate, but we all knew otherwise. That's what upset the mistress. She'd always hated that common, being so near.'

'So that's when they barred the gate,' I said.

With me, objects are associated with certain situations, and for ever afterwards I should never see that entrée dish which Gibby now turned absently in her hands, rubbing it back to brightness, without thinking of a scrawny young girl in maid's uniform, staring out of this same kitchen window at two policemen coming up through the shrubbery bearing a body. On what, I wondered? A plank? I was painfully excited, held fast by the fact that Gibby was my one link with those days. If I hadn't come back, she might have died before she could tell me. The old deserve respect and attention, for within themselves they contain living history. Without the old the young can hold no clues to their own identity.

So she had told me, and there was no cataclysm. Two women sitting in a kitchen on a rainy autumn day, talking about a tragedy that was over and done with long ago. After all, there was a tragedy in every family, and this was ours. The dead man had bequeathed it to us; the puzzle of it, the notoriety. But it was nonsense to go on gnawing at the bare bones for ever! Why should the Braithwaites do so? Why nurture the memory of it so that it grew like Jack's beanstalk and gradually darkened all the windows of The Hollies?

But I knew the answer even as I asked myself. It cut across their conception of themselves; it made them like other people, the terrible unknowable people who lived across the common. People whose names got in the papers.

'Did it ever get in the papers?'

Gibby looked as if I had struck her.

'Papers? 'Course not. Only the accident. They put that in. Things were different then, and they wouldn't 'a dared to come nosing around a family like this. There was talk, that's natural; and Gwennie did her share of that, so the mistress told her to pack her bags and go. She'd had trouble with her in other ways, too. The cheek of that girl passes understanding. Trying on the mistress's furs and telling lies when she was caught. . . .'

'What sort of lies?'

Gibby seized a meat dish and attacked it with fury. My question was idly put, but some instinct was at work and before she shut off from that time I wanted every drop of information I could squeeze out of her. After all, I knew very little about my grandfather, and she hadn't entirely filled the gap. I had a feeling that something was missing. Gibby was cunning, had she really come clean? She did an odd thing now. She whistled through her teeth, and it had the angry sound of an old dog being baited.

She said grimly, 'Gwennie told lies about the master, and for that I shall never forgive her, never, not if she came across that floor to me on her bended knees. And him dead and buried, with a certificate to say his gun had gone off accidental. Target practice he was at, the mistress said, he'd set up a target on that wall at the bottom of the garden. Used to spend hours there, firing with blanks. That morning he fell on his gun. And that's good enough for anyone.'

'But what was he doing outside the gate? Why are you so sure he meant to do it, Gibby?'

'He would never have spoilt the garden for his children, that's why. He loved his garden, did the master. So he walked out on to that old common, where it didn't matter. . . .'

'But —'

'Yes, I dessay it's hard for you to understand, but he was a top shot, won prizes for shooting. I've cleaned his silver cups and so have you. He knew the difference between a blank and a bullet, believe me. And a man what falls on his gun doesn't get the bullet through his brains clean as a

74

whistle. Everything clean and tidy. I've never known such a finicky man. Always washing, he was. Clean linen to his body, sometimes twice a day. He'd never die messy, not him!'

That clean, finicky man opening the gate; did he look back at the house? Loading the gun, setting it neatly to his head, judging his fall into the damp ditch so as not to contaminate his own ground . . . Say twenty paces outside? Then the shot, the collapse, the soft kicking; then peace. He was more alive to me now than he had ever been. I wanted to handle his books, examine a photograph, look deeply into the aunts' faces, into my own, for we were of his blood.

'Speaking ill of the dead,' Gibby was saying, 'that's what needled me. Wicked girl, I hope she ended on the streets. That's where she was heading.'

'Who – Gwennie? What did she say, Gibby?'

'Your Auntie Rosa caught her trying on your grandma's furs, as I told you. Dabbing away with eau-de-Cologne as well, she was, and she said the master liked her in furs; it made her nice and cuddly —'

'But was this before he died?'

'Oh yes. But she said as much afterwards. She never forgave Miss Rosa for slapping her face. You could see the marks for days. Always had a temper, Miss Rosa, under that soft look of hers. As if the master would look twice at a girl like that, a gentleman like him, with six children! It was a pity you never knew him, Miss Lou. He was a lovely man, and clever, too.'

Not so clever, I thought, and started on an over-embossed silver fruit-bowl with a soft brush.

'Miss Seraphina's coming,' said Gibby, and tightened her mouth into a button. I had heard nothing, but a moment later the door opened and Aunt Seraphina came in.

'You're cosy in here,' she said. 'I'll put the kettle on for a cup of tea. Oh, I don't know what your grandfather would say, Lou, if he could see his study now. A bed in it, just think!'

She came back from the scullery and sank down on to Gibby's hide sofa. She looked tired and old, and this made me feel sorry and guilty together, having made Gibby betray one of her secrets. What strange illusion was she clinging to, now? Why couldn't I say straight out, 'Look, I know, and it doesn't matter. It wasn't your fault, your sin; expiation isn't for you.' Calculating, I made her about fifteen when it happened. Hadn't she been set on an operatic career abroad? I know she had a year in Italy, studying; then she came home and stayed. My father was right; she had been a victim. The bullet had killed more than one person that misty autumn morning; I supposed it *was* autumn, but perhaps I was overplaying the present season to build up my own picture. One could never be sure where truth began. A fact, truth, might be like a black note of music, having certain values of its own, but dependent upon its place on the ruled lines for its effect.

On impulse I got up and put my arms round her. She did not respond, for neither of my aunts liked being touched, and now she was dry and stiff and surprised. At once I felt the hollowness of the gesture. If only she would break down and weep and wring her hands! For now Gibby, the talk having poured from her, looked different; gently smiling, human and pliable as I remembered her. Almost as if she had been made love to. I moved away to set out cups, and was horribly aware that Aunt Seraphina had never been made love to, if one could believe her about herself and Bruno; and one could. But Bruno was dead and now no man came to the house. Three dry old women dominated by the dead, and even Gibby would have forgotten what a man's touch was like.

The kettle whistled its way into the present, but instead of making the tea, I took out the whistle and made some excuse to go out of the room. At the telephone in the hall I was asking for Max's number when the front door opened and Aunt Rosa came in, shaking rain off her umbrella.

Without thinking, I at once replaced the receiver as the bell began to ring in the flat.

NINE

THE PANIC DECISION to telephone Max passed, and I was grateful for my aunt's timely entrance. I think she scarcely noticed me by the telephone as she came in complaining of the rain and shaking out her umbrella before placing it carefully in the stand, where it made puddles as she took off her coat.

'Ah, thank you, dear,' she said, as I eased the coat from her shoulders. 'Lucy Protheroe is failing, I'm afraid.' She unpinned her violet velvet toque and patted her short white hair. She pushed the long ruby-headed pin back into the hat with a shake of her head. 'Repeats herself so, poor soul. I hope I shall keep all my wits about me until they put me in the long box.'

'I'm sure you will, Aunt Rosa,' I said comfortingly. 'Now let me bring you a cup of tea. We're making one in the kitchen.'

'I'll go and rest in the little morning-room, dear. I left a fire there. I must put my feet up; it's quite a pull up Chestnut Crescent, you know. If you'd bring me a cup, yes, thank you. Poor Lucy's failing, I'm afraid. She does repeat herself so these days.'

She went off, shaking her head, and I went back to the kitchen to drink my tea while I finished off the brass. I hated doing these twisted candlesticks; they were so useless and made one's arm ache. Gibby had slipped out her bottom set of teeth, and I took it the way it was intended. As soon as I had polished the big inkstand Aunt Seraphina and I took it, with the candlesticks, into the study. They stood, rather grandly, quite without purpose on the desk.

'We'd better move Sir Roger,' I said.

'Yes. Cissie never liked him. She said he had fleas and insulted her. Nonsense, of course. It wasn't just her he insulted.'

I ran a finger along the wire of Sir Roger's tall Victorian cage. Inside, he swayed on his perch, and I almost expected him to brace himself and ruffle his wings to keep balance. But a dead bird, a stuffed parrot, could do no such thing.

Sir Roger, in his prime, had been a very fine parrot indeed. Pink and grey and full of character, he had outlived more than a dozen Braithwaites. No one knew exactly how old he was but he had been with the family – alive and dead – fifty years. I believe my grandfather had him from a friend in the City whose son had been overseas, and brought him home as a present for an unappreciative mother. I remembered him well because, after my parents died, we used to walk round the garden together, and I would coax him to talk to me. It bothered me to see him attempt to fly, with his clipped wings. I thought it unfair, so I would put him up in a tree and pretend he was a proper flying bird. Although I taught him several sentences, it seemed that his head was full of the phrases my grandfather had drummed into him. The aunts told me that he used to read to Sir Roger by the hour, alone in his study, and that the bird was almost capable of holding a conversation. They said that it was a miracle the bird's brain didn't burst, with all the bits of French and Latin and long passages from Milton that it had memorized. One day, however, so they said, it did.

I was at school when it happened, and returned to find the house shrouded. My grandmother had gone off to see the vicar, Gibby told me; the aunts were lying down. In those days she came in three days a week, because she was married to Fred and bringing up Nigel. The other days other women filled in for her. But Gibby was really in charge, and I was glad she was there that awful afternoon. I didn't see how a parrot's brain could burst, and when I asked my botany

mistress, she said it was an old wives' tale. Obviously the
bird had died of old age. I believed her, but I did not tell my
aunts this. They were engaged in battle with the vicar over
the burial. My grandmother wanted the vault opened, and
Sir Roger put inside.

'He was my husband's great companion,' she told him.
'It would be sacrilege to put him in a hole in the garden.
Can't you just sprinkle some holy water over his little coffin
and say a kind word or two?'

'We are not living in the days of the Pharaohs, Mrs
Braithwaite,' the poor man had retorted, extremely put out.
'I consider that a heathenish suggestion, if you will excuse
my speaking so plainly.'

'If *I* don't object to a parrot in my family vault, where I
shall be joining it in God's good time, then why should
you?' My grandmother could put up a fight like no one else,
Gibby told me. 'Remember the Crusaders' dogs. You've
seen them as footrests. At least I have, in Canterbury
Cathedral.'

The vicar was firm. Times had changed since the Crusades
and having a parrot in the Braithwaite vault might lead to
all sorts of abuses in his churchyard. He was sorry. He tried
to be jocular; but I can imagine the effort failing in the face
of three determined, hostile women. At last he suggested
that as they were so fond of the bird, it should be stuffed
and kept in its cage. People often did this, and he knew an
excellent taxidermist.

This in the end was what they did, to the vicar's relief and
his well-concealed surprise. Sir Roger stayed in grandfather's
study, his glass eyes now fixed unblinkingly on visitors,
his plumage dimly gleaming, one claw uplifted; alas, his
scissor voice was silent. The vicar was not allowed the last
word, however, Aunt Seraphina saw to that. She com-
missioned a little monument in stone, a sculptured effigy of
Sir Roger, and perched it on the flat lid of the vault, to act as

a rain-spout, like a gargoyle. Then, in the politest possible way, she dared the vicar to object. He did not. For one thing the family were regular churchgoers, and loyally supported all appeals, from the crumbling sacristy to needy choristers' outings. For another, the bird was functional, and attracted a great many visitors to the churchyard, and therefore to the church; but he did not encourage the reputation for eccentricity which the family gathered around itself, and came down very heavily on me in Sunday school for undue pride.

I took the cage from the round ebony table where it had stood for so many years, and my aunt put a bowl of fruit in its place.

'It was a strange name for a bird, Aunt Seraphina,' I said, knowing that my grandfather had named him; and everything about him was interesting to me that day.

'Your grandfather was a friend of Sir Roger Casement,' said Aunt Seraphina. 'He came here once when I was a girl. He was a fine-looking man, Sir Roger. He had just been knighted, and your grandfather asked whether he minded having the bird named after him. He was very taken with the idea. Sir Roger liked parrots. He brought a blue macaw back from the tropics for the Cadburys you know, and it escaped through the window of the train when he was taking it to Birmingham. It caused quite a stir.' Adding, as an afterthought, 'What a mercy your grandfather never lived to see his disgrace. Fancy hanging a fine-looking man like that! I never believed he was a traitor, whatever people might say, and however black things seemed. Never speak ill of the dead, Louise.'

She touched the bird's head gently through the bars.

'Cissie wanted to have the bird put away when all that scandal came out. But your grandfather would have said that he had enemies in high places. That's what it was – enemies in high places.' She rearranged the fruit in the bowl with little lost touches. 'But then I don't pretend to know anything about politics. Cissie never liked him after that, and he seemed to know it. He would scream in her ear.' She laughed, and to keep her in a good humour I took the cage and, putting my head near Sir Roger's, gabbled in a passable imitation of his throaty voice:

'What's the weather like outside, then? Hellish dark and smells of cheese!'

Encouraged by what I took to be a high-pitched giggle from my aunt, I tried out a phrase that I had read somewhere in connection with Casement's trial, 'Condemn a man with a semi-colon and hang him with a full-stop! Swing high, poor Sir Roger, swing —'

A long, strong hand was put over my mouth and I was looking, shocked, into Aunt Seraphina's blazing eyes. Fear had whitened her mouth.

'Don't. Don't. Don't,' she said, biting out the words and shaking her head. She reminded me of an old Spanish peasant woman we had once seen, lost in some grief unknown to us, outside her hut on a hot dry day years ago. Then she took her hand away and levered herself down into a chair. 'Don't ever do that again. You gave me, oh, such a fright. I thought —'

'The dead don't speak,' I said, not moving, not touching her. I was frightened myself, and my mouth hurt where she had driven my lips up against my teeth. 'I'm only speaking for him before he's banished. Shall I fetch the sal volatile?'

She was still a dreadful colour, but she made a violent gesture of refusal, so that all I could do was to stand and look at her, and hope that she would pull herself together. (That was a favourite phrase of hers, and I used it to myself, sadly, out of habit; it sounded so bleak, so alone, as if a puppet was in charge of its own strings which it had temporarily lost behind its back.) So we remained, she sitting, I standing, the cage in my hand, both in a state of shock. For if she had been unprepared for Sir Roger's farewell, I had certainly not expected a hand to be clapped so ruthlessly over my mouth. Physical violence had never been part of my life.

These thoughts ran in my mind as I stood there like the stone effigy of the cause of our upset. It was as if we had awakened something in that room, something that had been silent for a very long time.

My aunt seemed to be recovering. She straightened up like a tough blade of grass trodden down by some careless walker. If she suffered alone, she recovered alone, and this made me feel all the more guilty at having caused her pain. Even if she had deceived me.

'I'm so sorry, Aunt Seraphina,' I said. 'I didn't mean to give you such a fright. I thought you'd laugh.'

'Ah, Louise, we'll forget it, shall we? I'm sure you didn't mean it. Just thoughtless, that's all —' She stood looking round at the room with a little frown and, illogically, I felt I had never belonged to the family so completely. If I had hit her over the head she would still have found an excuse for me. You see, Max? I said silently, with triumph. They truly love me because I am of their blood. I don't have to do anything, be anything. I am myself. One of them. They don't need me to tell them I love them, and they don't need to tell me. We never say what we really mean in this house. Perhaps that is true communication.

'Now this room, Louie,' said my aunt, briskly. 'There's still something wrong. It wants a touch of something . . . oh, do put down that cage, dear. . . . Pictures, I wonder?'

The sun, out after the rain and sinking fast, touched the glass doors of the bookcases that lined the panelled walls. 'Does Cissie like pictures? I forget. I wish we didn't have to put her in here at all; but in a wheelchair where else can she go?' She looked out of the window on to the terrace and gave her characteristic click with her tongue against her upper teeth. It conveyed a good deal more than words. As they grew older I had noted a whole new field of expressive

83

comment opening up to the aunts as well as to Gibby, and this linked them with the children they had once been. Breathy sighs, huffs through the nose, a quick 'tch' of the upper lip.

'Anyway,' she went on absently, 'she has a splendid view of the garden. I hope she still cares for gardens. She's never been much of a reader, but we can't take the books out. Your grandfather was a great reader; we were a disappointment to him, I fancy. And Bertie never read. Poor Alec was the one. But I really think he enjoyed reading Voltaire to Sir Roger more than anything. He kept so still and quiet, as if he understood.'

I looked round the room. The bed looked wrong, of course, and the wardrobe, which we had brought down with a great to-do from Aunt Cissie's room upstairs. It reminded me of the furnished rooms Max and I had rented years ago, when it was obvious that we were living in one-fourth of someone's drawing-room, hastily partitioned. But the fire in the grate, the massive desk and carved chairs gave it a certain dignity. To make amends, I said cheerfully that we could go up to the attics and look out some pictures, and Aunt Seraphina responded at once, pleased with the idea.

'We'd better put poor Sir Roger up there while we're about it,' she said. As I took him up she gave him a long look and I could see that an idea was forming in her mind. I hoped she was not going to suggest that I should have him.

'Now, you naughty bird,' she said, in the intimate baby-talk she used to the cat, when she remembered it, 'we're going in to say bye-bye to Rosa.' And before I could prevent her, she had pushed me down the passage, across the hall, and had flung open the door of the little morning-room, where Aunt Rosa was resting. She hissed in my ear, 'Go on, go on, give her a fright! Talk like Sir Roger. It's a scream!'

Astonished, I half-heartedly thrust the cage round the

door and gabbled hoarsely, '*Vénus toute entière à sa proie attachée.* That's good, eh? I spy you there. I spy you there. Good-bye then, Miss and Madam, good —'

A cushion, flung with powerful accuracy from somewhere in the room, hit the cage and crashed it out of my hand. Behind me, Aunt Seraphina clutched her stomach, doubling up with loud painful hoots of laughter. Sir Roger lay in the bottom of his cage, his balance broken.

Scared of both of them, I went in, ready to ward off another cushion. But Aunt Rosa, very red in the face, merely stood at bay behind the sofa. She was very angry indeed, but not at all frightened. Her temper was evidently up.

'I'm surprised at you, Louise, I really am. You know my heart's bad . . . and tell Fina to stop that frightful noise! How anyone can think it funny I don't know.' Outside in the hall Aunt Seraphina's hysterical laughter had toned down; she was now moaning with the aftermath, and I felt my lips twitch in sympathy.

'We're just taking Sir Roger upstairs, you see. But I'm terribly sorry if —'

'Sorry! How old are you? And Fina, how could you encourage the child to get up to such tricks? Now go away, for pity's sake. And take that – that damned bird with you!' Her pale blue eyes seemed to expand behind her spectacles, and she tottered round the sofa without her shoes. She had taken them off to put her feet up, obviously, and must have moved like an athlete at Sir Roger's words. I hadn't made them up. I had often heard him say them; they had come naturally. Why had they affected her so strongly? Or was it, I pondered, as I carefully shut the door in chastened stealth, and followed my other aunt to the stairs, was it merely the suddenness of hearing an unexpected voice? It would shock anybody, after all.

Aunt Seraphina hiccuped all the way up to the third landing. Then she stopped, leaned against the banister and said she wished she'd seen Rosa throw that cushion. 'Straight as a die, wasn't it? And only one eye. She's a marvel.' Then she remembered Aunt Rosa's words and burst out indignantly, 'Tricks! I'll trick her one day, my girl! She's played enough tricks on me in her time.'

As we went slowly up the wooden flight to the attics, I said, 'Oh yes. Gibby was telling me that she was a great tease. She tried to throw a doll of yours out of the window, didn't she?'

'She tried to, because she was jealous. Dada gave it to me. Sweetly pretty it was. Bertie stopped her. And Nurse Higgs gave her such a smack and sent her to her room. The great Miss Braithwaite didn't like that at all. Even mama threatened her with the hairbrush if she didn't behave. She was always tormenting us younger ones.' She seemed beside herself; her thin face was working. The past had laid a clammy hand on her that afternoon, and I regretted again that Aunt Cissie's arrival should throw us all into such an upheaval.

'Cissie was as bad,' she went on, as if guessing my thought. 'It was always one or the other. I tell you, my girl, I'm in the book, but I don't know what page I'm on. And who looked after them all, *and* their children? The boys went. I never married. Not me – I never had a chance. What have I got to show for it now?'

She sat down abruptly on the wooden stairs and looked at me, markedly. For a moment I felt sick, as if this was a question I had to answer; for her, for myself, for them all. The empty attics above us, the empty rooms below, the deserted, ghost-ridden garden: all these contained the answer, and it was a cold one. *Yet all shall be well, all manner of things shall be well.* If I believed this, I could say the words to her, but I was dumb. We had never spoken about spiritual comfort: it was a subject as taboo as money.

To my relief the moment passed. She stood up; said quite

sharply, 'So Gibby told you. When? She's such a chatter-box.'

'We were talking of this and that, you know how it is. She's devoted to you both. She loves to talk about the old days.' I embroidered, reminding Aunt Seraphina of family jokes; talking of Bertie in the garden, of Aunt Sue. So we went on up to the first attic, and the dangerous moment was past.

I put the cage on the floor. Once a maid had slept here, with the gurgle of pipes that was not supposed to disturb the lower classes. Now it held trunks and boxes and old chairs. Somewhere, under drifts of tissue paper, was my mother's wedding dress. White satin, and imitation lilies of the valley.

'I suppose I'd better cover him up,' I said, looking at the parrot on the floor of his cage, feeling a curious compunction. 'Poor Sir Roger. I've never heard a better talker, have you, Aunt Seraphina? But what a ghastly French accent. . . .'

She was over by a domed trunk, her head inside, so she did not hear me. But in a moment she came across with a piece of faded cretonne, an old chair cover. We put it over the cage with some ceremony, in silence, and that was Sir Roger's long good night.

TEN

THAT EVENING, perhaps because Aunt Cissie's arrival would prevent them from indulging for a matter of weeks, even months, the aunts slid imperceptibly into what as a child I had privately called 'the Game'. In my grand-mother's time they had often played it, believing that it was she who was being indulged. It might have been that my aunt's visit to the attics, and all those old boxes of photographs she had found, had brought the past back so vividly that she was compelled to give it body. Whatever it was, as soon as I had helped Gibby with the washing up, and my aunts and I sat round the fire, Aunt Seraphina said:

'Louise found Gordon's suitcase up in the attics, Rosa. Do you remember the tennis parties we used to have with the Wilson boys? There are lots of snaps.'

Aunt Rosa gave her a sharp look. Her plump, pink face with its blue eyes could close up like a satin purse. Now, as she glanced over to me, her glasses reflected the light from the rose-shaded standard lamp, and the special lens she wore to help the sight of her one good eye, magnified the eyeball alarmingly. Under all her softness she was indeed for-midable, and although she had recovered from her anger and shock of the afternoon, she held herself away from us. During the evening she would break off pieces of forgive-ness, like cake, and hand them to us.

'Gordon's suitcase? That old thing? Snaps? Photographs, you mean, Seraphina. Snaps indeed. Such an unsuitable word, especially at your age.'

Poor Aunt Seraphina looked rebuked; she was given to using out-of-date slang terms, which she thought kept her young and in touch. All the same, 'snaps' did not seem very slangy to me, but I said nothing. To show her disapproval still further Aunt Rosa went on, 'I don't expect there was much else in it. The boy hadn't much to leave. I still can't get over those shares.'

'I don't know anything about my father's family,' I said, stung. 'Where did they come from?'

Aunt Rosa looked restlessly round the room and spoke sharply, 'Pull the curtains, Louise. Let's shut the night out. What did you say? Oh, the Potters? His mother was Welsh, I believe. But they were nobodies; we never had much to do with them. A sister came to the funeral, and we never saw her again.'

So much for my father. I saw that this spitefulness had almost cleansed her of her displeasure, and returning from the window, I handed her several photographs. As she looked at them, holding them well away, Aunt Seraphina said sympathetically:

'Gordon was a deep one. A gentleman, though. I often wondered what he thought about all day, lying out there.'

I could have told her, but I said nothing, holding his letter fast in my mind, untouched, safe. It was beginning to have its effect, like a pain wearing off but leaving the knowledge behind, so that one was never quite the same again. The aunts had shifted, ever so slightly, out of focus.

Aunt Rosa said now, letting the photographs lie in her lap:

'Fancy you finding those pictures of dada's. I think they look very pretty in Cissie's room.'

'Cissie's room? The study, you mean.'

'I mean Cissie's room. It *is* Cissie's room now, I suppose?'

'That means she has two rooms.' Aunt Seraphina put down the album she was leafing through and frowned. 'I think, Rosa, we should make it clear to her that she is only in dada's study because of her health. It wouldn't do, otherwise.'

'Whatever do you mean, Fina? Wouldn't do, indeed! I

don't see that it hurts you for her to have two rooms. She can't use them both at the same time, can she? This is a big house, and after all, it is her home.'

To stop the rapidly developing quarrel, I said quickly:

'I thought at first those watercolours had been painted by grandmother.'

'Your grandmother never had time,' exclaimed Aunt Seraphina at once.

'No, she was too busy with the children. Painting pictures, that's a funny idea for mama. Can *you* see her painting pictures, Fina?'

They both gave short laughs, as if the prospect of their mother sitting down and doing anything other than mending or knitting or perhaps petit point was out of the question. But the pictures had interested me profoundly. There was a delicate strength about them; and it was difficult to believe that a man had done them.

We had found them in the wicker hamper, with a great many framed portraits and large Victorian landscapes of solid sepia splendour. They were not large, and were framed in gilt. They were paintings of flowers; sections cut through the whole flower head, sometimes whole plants. Cuckoo pint, orchids, an unusual lily, pomegranates. There was a faintly text-book air about them; one expected the parts to be labelled. They were not pretty, but practical, as if there was some positive reason for painting them. He had never done anything else, I had found out as much from my aunt. They were somehow disquieting, and I would have liked to show them to Max, to have his opinion.

The aunts were involved in a discussion about the Wilson boys, so I knew they were on the verge of the Game, at last.

The Game had started many years ago, in my grandmother's time. Then it had begun as a joke. Sometimes, as I sat doing my homework in the corner of the drawing-room, Aunt Seraphina would say, 'Do you remember that little dress of Sue's, mama? The one she wore to the Anderson's party when she was six? I saw a piece of material just that colour today. I nearly bought it to make a blouse for Louise.'

My grandmother's head would jerk up into her listening attitude, making a beautiful curve of her arched nose and long neck. She might say, 'Sue wore a yellow tussore to the Andersons' party, if you mean the *Christmas* party. You ought to remember, Seraphina, because you made it yourself, with all those tucks. Now I do pride myself on my memory, and I'm sure it was the yellow tussore. You must be thinking of the year after, the Anderson girl's *birthday*.'

'The yellow tussore was a *summer* dress, mama. Sue wore it to the Vicarage garden party. Surely you remember? With white silk socks and a matching bow. She carried that little sunshade, the cream one I brought back from Italy. Everyone who saw her said —'

I would listen, fascinated, my homework forgotten. This long-dead aunt, the little girl, Susan, came alive before me, pirouetting in her yellow tussore dress – or was it the red silk? In these exchanges Aunt Seraphina and my grandmother came nearer than love. But it shocked me, for I knew that there was malice in my aunt's words; she found supreme entertainment in her mother's failing memory.

But what had started as a little private baiting became, with time, a contest. The odd thing was that it sharpened my grandmother's memory, as Pelmanism was supposed to do, and she sometimes bested my aunt, slamming down an unexpected trump card.

'Sue wore a red bow to the pantomime the Robinsons took her to, the Christmas you had chicken-pox.' Although they sometimes chose other children, other incidents from the past, it was this red bow I always remembered when I thought about the Game.

'Pink, mama,' Aunt Seraphina returned, quick as a player calling 'Snap!'

'Red, my girl, red. I still have that piece upstairs, in the trunk with my remnants. I was looking out something for Louie the other day and came across it. I bought that length when I was shopping at Gorringes for Mary's trousseau.'

Pause. Aunt Seraphina never cheated, I'll say that for her. She dared not cheat the living past. Grandmother pressed the point home.

'She couldn't wear pink with that cherry velvet dress.'

'Ah. Yes, it was red, then.'

Game to grandmother. And she would start to hum a little song. Then (for she too was scrupulously fair) she might give Aunt Seraphina a lead.

'Have you still kept that pretty green shot-silk dress you wore to your first grown-up party? You looked a picture in that.'

Pause. I would stop in the middle of my English essay to hear what my aunt had to say. This time she did not hesitate.

'I cut it down for Sue two years later. It suited her even better, being so dark. She wore it to the —'

'The Protheroes!' cried my grandmother, 'And —'

'And she had a cold, so we wrapped her up in Rosa's red velvet cloak —'

'With ermine on the hood —'

'*Lined* with ermine; Rosa got it cheap from Bradley's —'

'And the snow stood so high we could scarcely open the front door. . . .'

I watched them in astonishment, being unused to such complete agreement and, to my horror, surprised tears in their eyes as they looked at each other. The child stood in their minds, dressed for the party, the favourite, the last born, holding her shoes in a silk bag, in this very room. Vivid, dark, alive, with the beginnings of an unusual beauty. The nursemaid stood by, muffled up in some heavy coat, waiting for her to be handed over.

Then they fell silent and looked down at their neglected sewing. I, too, looked back to my work, and so we relinquished Sue: to the party, one of many that would come her way in the following years; relinquished her to marriage, to death in India at the age of barely thirty. Upstairs, her room stood ready, her photographs, her letters, the skins of the animals she had shot; crocodile for shoes and handbags still to be made up as presents for her sisters, skins of black monkeys, even a tiger rug. Dresses she had made for herself out of silk *saris* – for she was a skilled needlewoman – table mats woven by native children, elephant-hair bracelets, and cut-glass bottles with the faintest whiff of old scent about them. . . . But the door closed on all this. It was too much, and it was time for cribbage.

The photograph the aunts were arguing about was small and smudgy, but I made out a tall, thin man in baggy white flannels, handing round glasses of lemonade on his tennis racquet. He had the lopsided grin of the compulsive comic, and with him was a thin girl with a lot of hair and a long, shapeless dress that had once been the last thing for tennis. She was giving him a grotesque curtsy.

'That's you, playing the fool as usual, Fina,' Aunt Rosa gave a tiny shriek. 'And Bill Protheroe was quite a card in those days, wasn't he? So different now, poor man.'

They gave each other small, secretive smiles, then decided to include me.

'I refused him four times,' said Aunt Seraphina. 'Such a jolly man, but too much altogether. No – he never seemed quite, well – it would have been like living in a play. I preferred a more serious type. A man should be serious. Like dada.'

Aunt Rosa had laid Bill Protheroe face-down on the little table by her side. She was looking through a disordered pile of faded, curled-up photographs. The figures on them looked as if they were congealed in a pale sauce. One she picked up and handed to me.

'That was your Uncle Frank. It was taken on the day we were engaged. I have it in my own album upstairs; I didn't know there was another print.'

Two figures: Aunt Rosa in a wide-brimmed hat and with an incredibly small waist, the man beside her stiff-legged against her flowing skirts. They stood, each with a hand on an artificial pillar, while behind them the studio wall was adorned with wisteria. Uncle Frank looked as if he had been poured into his suit of clothes and set like plaster of Paris. I could see nothing to commend him.

'How handsome you both look!'

It was all I could say. It seemed impossible that Aunt Rosa had ever progressed from artificial pillar to marriage-bed with this young man whose moustache eclipsed his face. The whiff that came from this ancient romance was as stale as the air breathed out by Aunt Seraphina's bowls of pot pourri.

'It didn't last long,' said Aunt Rosa. 'He was killed in the war. But it was a love match.'

Pink, old, sexless and suddenly vulnerable, she sat there by the small late summer or early autumn fire, and I wanted to go down on my knees and hug her, just as I had wanted to hug Aunt Seraphina in the kitchen earlier that day. . . . I had always been prey to these sudden emotions, which were entirely un-Braithwaite and thought to be unladylike. They put it down to the Potter streak, a dangerous weakness in a seam of coal that might bring down the workings, but I could not help myself. Once I had heard my mother singing in an upstairs room. She had a light, pretty voice, and the song was called *Zigeune*, a yearning, sentimental song she loved to play on the piano. Young as I was, I had wanted to take up the nostalgic memory it had for her (I had no idea what it was); take up her love, her small triumphs, her innocent wants, and press them all gently into her hands. It was the same now; the old photographs, the Game trembling in the balance. I was outside the past they had lived through and I wondered passionately what it was like to be old, for the old savour the past, which is themselves at a different rate of living. They encompassed youth, and this made me feel brash and unfinished, quite at a disadvantage.

So I merely said, 'It was better than outgrowing love.'

'Oh, love!' she said, putting love in its place. 'One is glad of it, of course, but there are so many other things. What have you there, Fina?'

'Bertie, the summer he shaved off his moustache. It must be – no, there's no date, how annoying – 1918.'

'1919. He shaved it off on Armistice Day, and that was in November. We couldn't have taken a photograph out-of-doors in the winter.'

'But he grew it again because he said it made him look older.'

'That wasn't until he went to Canada. I put it at 1919. Look, here's another. And see who's with him! M. Ducharry of all people. The light got in the camera, so the whole roll of film must be affected. They must all have been taken at the same time.'

'Here's mama with M. Ducharry. Doesn't she look pleased!'

'That proves it's 1927. The Ducharrys spent the summer with us, don't you remember? Here's Susan with the eldest boy.'

While they were turning over the photographs with excited pleasure, I took up the one of my grandmother with M. Ducharry. Then, to compare, I ruffled through another album until I found one of her in youth. A yellowed, studio portrait. Then one in age, a snapshot in the rose arbour, with me by her knee.

She had a strong face, with a bold, narrow nose and a clear, thrusting jaw. The kind of face that weathered flawlessly into age, so that people remarked on what a beauty she must have been when young. But beauty had not touched this face in youth. Then it had a raw and flinching look, the proud nose somehow emphasizing the self-conscious hunted expression of the large, clear and vulnerable blue eyes. In the studio portrait they looked like the bolting eyes of a rabbit. Looking further, turning the stiff cardboard pages with the little revealing windows set in the centre, I saw one of her taken at someone's wedding, perhaps in anonymous middle age. High-collared, the hair hideously puffed at the temple, flanked by daughters whose hats dipped extravagantly with feathers. Here she was handsome but featureless. Perhaps it was the occasion.

I looked again at the snapshot taken with M. Ducharry, of whom I had heard from time to time. She must have been ill. She looked fine-drawn, her eyes hollowed, her hair flat, drawn over the ears. But here she approached beauty, for the eyes had seen suffering, the face had come to terms with life, and the terms had been forced upon it. Will, the unthinking female will, had begun to realize that certain things must be accepted. This face – unless I was reading too much into it – had begun to be aware that other people's failings were perhaps her own, rebounding. This face had known love. What had happened in my grandmother's middle age to make such a difference? I did not really have to ask myself. I was sure. All the same, I remarked casually:

'What a charming man, M. Ducharry! Was he an old friend of the family?'

Aunt Rosa looked up to say, 'We met him on holiday at

Dinard. He was a widower. He was very struck with mama. The idea!'

'Oh, it might have been lovely if they had married!' I exclaimed, with idiotic ingenuousness. 'Think of it: you could all have been brought up in France!'

'Mama would never have dreamed of marrying a second time. And certainly not a foreigner. He had four children of his own.'

'We never liked them. French children are so precocious,' said Aunt Seraphina. 'And M. Ducharry was quite officious after mama's breakdown. That was when he stayed a whole summer with us. I mean, of course, he stayed at an hotel. He called almost every day.'

'He wanted to take Sue back with him, to perfect her French. He asked us, too. But we never went. I had my work, and Fina had mama to look after. But Sue did go one summer. She loved him. Came back speaking French like a native.'

'Didn't he —'

'We never saw him again. And to tell the truth, dear, it was a relief. It wouldn't have done at all. I'm sure he merely embarrassed mama. Anyway, she refused to discuss it with us.'

'Still, Rosa, we let her know how we felt.'

I was sure they had.

It was strange how this family had shed its men. They lost them by illness and disaster. And, if I faced it, by desertion. For their brothers, except for Bertie, still, one presumed, in Canada or America, were dead. They outlived their husbands, would-be lovers, and sons. Men, one felt, were merely milestones.

I no longer wanted to play the Game; suddenly it filled me with dread. I didn't want to live in a world where men were expendable. I got up.

'I think I'll go out for a breath of air,' I said. 'The rain's stopped.'

'You've upset the box, dear,' said Aunt Rosa.

I rose to pick up the scattered photographs, hating them. They were like so many tombstones; they were silent like Sir Roger up in the attic. But as I put them back, one stared up at me. A flashlight one, full of faces. Champagne glasses caught the light, and the glare of magnesium had flattened the faces into mere eyes and mouths. Everyone was laughing and seemed to be crowding around a table on which stood a flower, a lily of sorts, with trumpet-shaped blooms that were familiar. Next to it, looking wildly excited, was my grandfather. He was toasting it; obviously it was some sort of triumph. Next to him, my grandmother, looking down, her hand on his arm. My grandfather's eyes were wide open; he was staring at the camera, as if to challenge it. His teeth showed in a laugh that was almost a snarl, and his eyes, as I looked, seemed to blaze. I felt very cold.

'What have you got there, Louie?' asked Aunt Seraphina, and I turned the picture over to see. In my grandmother's hand was written 'The night of the *Keng hua* party.' The date was indecipherable.

I read this out and handed the photograph to them.

They stared at it without a word, then turned it over and read the faded words for themselves.

'Whose hand is this? It looks like mama's. But —' Aunt Rosa's voice was so cracked I scarcely recognized it.

'I thought she had destroyed it.'

'You look as if you're celebrating something. What was it, Aunt Seraphina?'

Aunt Seraphina seemed to shrivel. She said slowly. 'It was to celebrate the blooming of the *Keng hua* lily. It was a rare Chinese lily. Dada and I raised it together, and I believe it was the first time it had ever bloomed in this country. It went on blooming all night, Louie, you never saw such a sight! From eight o'clock until midnight – the flowers unfolding one after the other. They faded at about four in the morning. Dada said that in China people held parties to celebrate such a thing, for some lilies only bloom once in a hundred years. I don't know whether —'

Aunt Rosa tore the photograph in two and threw it into the fire.

'Don't chatter, Seraphina. Louise, will you fetch the brandy from the dining-room? I think a small night-cap will do us all good.'

Her face looked bluish and, remembering her heart, I went quickly and fetched the decanter and glasses. As I came back, Aunt Seraphina met me in the corridor outside and whispered, clutching my arm:

'It made her sad, that's why she's so queer. Dada died soon after the party. It was the last photograph ever taken of him.'

She followed me back into the room. Aunt Rosa sat with her hands folded in her lap. She was speaking to herself, shaking her head from side to side, oblivious of us.

'Is nothing ever done with? Does nothing ever finish?'

'I think I'll go out now,' I said loudly. 'I'll take the door-key, so that I won't disturb you.'

Aunt Seraphina poured the brandy into two of the three glasses and said, in consternation:

'But it's after ten! You can't walk the streets at this hour: it isn't safe for a young girl. Why don't you just take a turn up the terrace instead?'

Aunt Rosa said nothing.

'I feel like a walk. I feel restless. After all, I slept all the morning. Don't worry; I won't be long.'

I kissed them both and left them to their brandy and their memories. I went to my handbag and took out four pennies, slipped the doorkey into the pocket of my raincoat and was outside under the free night sky. I was sick to death of secrets.

ELEVEN

I WALKED QUICKLY. The exhausted remnants of the rain were being chivvied by a west wind which was blowing long strands of grey cloud over a high moon. They looked like disordered old-women's-hair, and they obscured the light. The fat hedges wet my hand as I brushed past them, and I went along the pavement, jumping over the lines. I told myself that if I got to the telephone-box without stepping on one, Max would be in.

I had to cheat, but it was worth it. He was in. It was his voice announcing the number, saying his name, then there was a pause. So there I was, connected as if by an umbilical cord to the present, to sanity. I felt at once relief and a resentment at feeling relief.

He said questioningly, patiently, 'Hullo?'

The telephone does things to people's voices. Like the radio, it finds one out. It is a kind of audio-X-ray, if there could be such a thing. Accents that people have been hiding for years come out into the light, with full distortion: it is a great betrayer of flattened vowels, of the rounded period, the self-congratulatory self-listener. It sharpens the nervous voice, and imperializes the bossy; it is a great test to lovers.

Max's voice was calm; you felt he was there in his own right. His calmness flowed to me over miles of wire. I could see him, sitting by the telephone, which was on the small table by our blue-covered divan. At once I wondered whether he was alone, whether he could talk.

'Max?' I said. 'It's —'

'Darling,' he said at once. 'How are you? Where are you? Are you coming home?'

He was less calm then than I imagined. There wasn't a hint of rancour, or hurt pride or blame. I might have been telephoning to say that I'd missed the last train and would be late. Merely this warmth, this acceptance of temporary distance.

'Well, no. I can't come home, not yet. Max, I've been finding out, well . . . Things have happened, and I —'

'Don't cry,' he said. 'Take a deep breath.'

Of course that made me cry, and it made me cross, too, being told to take a deep breath after I'd run away after all these years, and left a dramatic note. He —

I took a deep breath and sobbed out in fury, 'I'm not crying. I'm not a child. Are you alone?'

'Of course.'

There was a curious noise in my ear and, unbelieving, I held the receiver away.

'Max! How dare you, you're laughing!'

'Of course I'm laughing, you're such an idiot! How are your dragons one and two?'

I looked up into the little oblong mirror above the telephone and saw that although my eyes were a horrible sight, I was smiling.

'Number three arrives tomorrow. Max, do you know why I left you?'

'I've been thinking about nothing else. I've thought of a thousand reasons, but they don't fit you as I think I know you. You wouldn't leave me because you think I'm a failure – no, let me go on. If you really thought that, you'd stick. The Braithwaites love a martyr. But I must have failed *you*, in some way I don't know about: that's what hurts. Look, we can't talk over the phone, it's too silly. At least let's meet, and you can —'

The wind whipped up a handful of plane leaves and plastered them against the glass sides of the box I stood in. It was like being in a lighthouse among dark seas.

'But I feel freer on the telephone. I'm in a box at the end of the road. I can think when I'm alone like this. Just this box and the night outside and your voice coming out of nowhere . . . Can you understand?'

Max's voice was heavy with tiredness as he said, 'Yes, I understand. Go on.'

Go on? What could I tell him? How could I hand him the day, which had stretched so long from dawn until now? There had never been a longer one. I must try. I owed it to him. For instance, to begin with —

'Well, there was a letter from my father, you see. We've got, oh Max, isn't it wonderful, we've got seven hundred and fifty pounds. Out of the blue. I saw the solicitor. You'd hate him, he's like a rabbit with a pep pill. . . .'

It was no good; there was too much to tell.

'Lou – Louie, have *you* been at those pep pills again? You're talking nonsense.'

'What pep pills? You don't know anything about —'

'Louie, please. D'you think I'm blind? I know every mood of yours, drug-induced or normally manic. For God's sake. So you're living in the past. The vast secure womb of The Hollies. So how is it there? But don't talk to me about letters from your father. . . .'

'All right, I won't,' I said in a bitter rage, and slammed down the receiver. At once I looked for more money to ring again, but of course I had only brought fourpence with me. I opened the door of the booth and walked out. I was suddenly mortally tired, so tired that I could scarcely crawl home. Or should I say, crawl back to The Hollies. I didn't know where home was, and this thought crawled with me, and tired me to death, because it meant that one never finished the journey.

TWELVE

AUNT CISSIE ARRIVED, by taxi, the following afternoon, at tea-time. There was a wind. It had got up in the night, and brought with it a sea freshness, as if it had blown straight off the grey breakers, over the Sussex downs and into Pagham Green. It made one feel exhilarated and slightly mad. Everything in the garden sparkled after the rain, like the dark side of spring and I had gathered a great bunch of dahlias, which Aunt Seraphina had arranged with magnificent abandon in two porcelain urns. They gave the big polished hall a gala look.

The trees lashed in the high wind and Aunt Cissie cursed it as she was trundled up the curving drive and into the house, holding on to her fur toque. She had the eccentric look of minor royalty.

'What are *you* doing here, young woman?' she asked me, even before shooting out her cheek to be kissed by her sisters. 'Ah, Gibby, still alive, I see,' and nodded in a satisfied way, as if some private doubt had been cleared up.

'How are you, dear?' asked Aunt Rosa nervously. 'We've put you in dada's study, because of the stairs. Louise, push your aunt through into the drawing-room, will you?'

Aunt Cissie sat in her wheelchair, tiny and malevolent. She could not have weighed more than seven stone, and yet she seemed to vibrate with energy and fill the hall. I had forgotten, or perhaps had never noticed, how handsome she was. She had the Braithwaite nose, high and arched, and a look of a Basque woman about her: indomitable, aristocratic, and yet with a peasant's energy. Beside her, my two aunts looked faded. Aunt Rosa stood like some upper servant, reserved and discreet in dark-grey flannel; a tailored dress that emphasized her rosiness. Aunt Seraphina, more brittle than slim, had, in her nervousness, puffed pink powder over her face so that it settled in drifts under her eyes. I had forgotten to look her over before she came down. She had changed out of her gardening tweeds into a blue woollen dress. They felt bolstered up by their clothes. It would never do, Aunt Rosa had confided to me that morning, dropping a hint as to my own efforts, for Cissie to think that we had gone to seed.

'I can work this damned chair myself, thank you,' Aunt Cissie said now, in her strong, penetrating voice. 'I may be a cripple, but I'm not bedridden. How am I? Well, apart from this —' And she pulled up her long black and white tweed skirt to show a leg like a pencil caged in a steel caliper, and secured at knee, and presumably, for we did not see so far, at waist, by a leather strap. 'Apart from this, and a silver pin in my hip, I've never felt better. Idle, that's what I've been. Idle. *And* enjoying it. Beware the too active person, I say, who never has time to think. Oh, I'm all for the contemplative life now. What are you laughing at, Louise?'

Her light grey eyes, under bushy white eyebrows, shot in my direction like levelled guns. I had burst out laughing at the prospect of my small, volcanic aunt as a contemplative.

'You'll have plenty to read, then, in grandfather's study.'

'I'll go along and see it. Thank God we've got a downstairs lavatory. It makes everything so much easier.'

'Oh,' said Aunt Rosa, 'Oh . . . er . . . Cissie, can you manage? Shall I —'

'No thanks. I've cut my drawers through. I *can* walk with this thing on my hip, so I'm not helpless. But it's a bit heavy and the doctor tells me that if I go about on it, the bone will crumble.'

She put her fine little hands on the wheels and went spinning off along the hall passage, calling over her shoulder as she went:

'Just bring my cases, will you, Louise?'

Aunt Rosa shook her head, clicked her tongue, and her voice was admiring but wary as she spoke.

'She's a marvel. Wonderful girl. What grit!'

Aunt Seraphina looked after her with quite another expression. One I couldn't name, but I knew it was not congratulatory. However, she said nothing, and went off into the kitchen with Gibby to bring in the tea.

When I arrived in the study, or as I was coming to think of it, in Aunt Cissie's room, she was whirling round in her chair, looking at it from all angles.

'I see you've taken that damned bird away,' she said. 'What a relic! What a companion for a man to choose! And you've routed out your grandfather's pictures. What would he say, I wonder, if he could see me here? Hey?' Extreme pleasure changed her tone and she waved a hand towards her bed. 'Put the cases over there, please. Yes. Well. I must say they've taken a great deal of trouble. Not much else to live for at their age, I suppose. Old age is what you make it, but then you wouldn't know. Yet.'

A flash of pure malice shone from her tight little face. The flesh was very white and thin over fragile bones. She looked like a picked bird. I was amazed to find that I no longer feared her; her tartness was refreshing, and I felt free to say what had struck me the moment the door had opened to her.

'Aunt Cissie, you're better-looking now than I ever remember you.'

At once she wheeled herself across to the big gilt mirror we had hung on the wall opposite the door, looked into it, and flung her gloves straight into her reflection.

'Am I supposed to be grateful for that remark?' But she was pleased. 'How patronizing the young are! We Braith-waites wear well, that's certainly true. But what good does it do us?' She was looking into the mirror straight at me, critically. 'You'll be better-looking in middle-age, too. At the moment you look – now, how do you look? Muted. Yes, that's it. Muted.' She came across the room to me and with a surprisingly soft hand touched my cheek gently, here and there. 'These bones will come out and dramatize the eyes, you'll see. Then the nose – you've a fine nose, like me – the nose is thrown into prominence. That's when we should be painted, not in youth. And talking of painting, how's that husband of —'

Luckily the tea-bell rang. This was a touch the aunts kept only for visitors and I was just as startled as Aunt Cissie. 'I see we keep up our style on tuppence ha'penny a week, and one poor old woman of all work! What a world. Now I'll just wash, and then I'll be along. Don't you wait.'

'You'll find everything in the cloakroom,' I said. 'Except a bath.'

'*Cloakroom* now. I suppose that's what Fina calls it. I only see the word in suburban house-agent's lists. Ah well, never mind; the poorer they grow, the nicer their language. Thank God I've got money. You're no good old without it.' And she was out of the room and away.

It is strange the difference another person makes in the atmosphere of a house. Already I could feel something stirring, as if the house was in pain, flexing its arthritic joints. It would have to expand to absorb this new irritant.

I realized, as we sat at afternoon tea, with its lace and its fragile cups and its silver and its plum cake (for Gibby had splashed out to welcome Aunt Cissie) that this was the first visitor we had received since my return. Apart from Miss Protheroe and her brother, very few of the aunts' friends were alive. Every morning they read the obituary notices in *The Times*, and twice since my arrival they had retired after breakfast to write their letters of condolence to the grand-children or relatives of the deceased. Soon these childhood friends would feature in the Game. Two more playing-cards for their pack.

Perhaps, being known in youth and onwards was a protection in one's old age from the ultimate, terrifying change. For there was, under the changing shape, the bag of skin, the sag of muscle and the curious quirks of increasing years, the essential living core, the nucleus. A look, a movement, could sparkle up; sparkled up now as I watched the three of them eating their cake with the innocent greed the very young share with the very old. This look made the physical cage a mere foolish encumbrance. But, I thought, people who had not known you in youth possessed no reference. To them you were as you appeared, and this was a terrible thing. I wondered whether this was the reason my aunts so seldom went out, so seldom entertained. It was as if they were running a film backwards. The circles made by the stone flung into the present no longer widened into concentricity, but instead contracted, narrowed, shrank back on to the place of plummeting entry. In our end is our beginning. 'I can only say, there we have been, but I cannot say where.'

Aunt Seraphina seemed to be in a state of abeyance. She was absorbing her sister's presence in order to marshal it into its proper place in the pattern of her life. Apart from her famous 'response', she had always loved to recreate a quite simple happening (an exchange with a bus conductor, a visit to a friend), in terms charged with high drama. Tinselled like a Christmas card, or made sinister with black edges, the event would be crowned, enlarged, exalted, the original distorted like the starting sentence in a children's game of whispers. I realized that Cissie, with her broken hip, her worldly airs, was not yet quite real to her.

The cause of her disturbance sat, replete but edgy, with an air of mocking restlessness, crackling like an electric storm. Of the three, Aunt Rosa, placid, pink-skinned, sat and smiled. She did no planning, either for the past or for the future. For her the present was enough. In fact, watching them through the wreaths of cigarette smoke, I saw them as past, present and future. Three goddesses who might yet show me the way.

'Haven't you a television?' asked Aunt Cissie, when Gibby came in to clear away. Only then did I realize that she was bored. Aunt Seraphina gave a short, hard bark through her nose.

'Certainly not. We couldn't possibly afford such a thing. Anyway, it's all low nonsense.'

'Allow me to be the judge of that. What rubbish you talk, Fina. What do you do with yourselves?'

'We have a wireless when we want it. We do our needlework. I look after the garden. We entertain ourselves as we have always done. Don't forget I play the piano and sing. As a girl —'

'You'd be better off in an hotel. Plenty of company there. Take mine, in Eastbourne. Concerts on the front. Television lounge. No meals to worry about. This house must eat up your incomes.'

'Ssh. Oh, do hush, Cissie!' Aunt Rosa was horrified. 'I'd die if I had to live in an hotel. We manage very well here, thank you.'

'We don't want any interference from you,' snapped Aunt Seraphina, seeing that it was safe to explode. 'I've never heard of such a thing! That's a terrible thing to say. Live in an hotel, indeed — and what would become of mama's house, may I ask, that we've kept up all these years?'

'Sell it,' said Aunt Cissie tersely. 'Sell it and enjoy yourselves.'

My two aunts and I were struck into utter silence by this monstrous remark. The very walls seemed to give a thin scream. For a moment I thought Aunt Rosa would attack her sister; the vision of that cushion, thrown with such force and accuracy the previous day, recurred. But, turning a mottled grey, she merely said, taking up her knitting with shaky hands, 'We know you're joking, Cissie. And please don't discuss money in front of the child.'

Aunt Cissie was about to take this up, and turned to me with open mouth, but I was not going to be her next target. Instead, I said, hastily, hardly thinking:

'I was wondering, as a matter of fact, Aunt Rosa, whether you and Aunt Seraphina would care to have a television set as a present from me. With the winter coming on, you might enjoy it. Some of the programmes are —'

'Keep your money, child. Keep it. You'll need it. And now, either turn on the wireless, Seraphina, or play the piano, for my head will burst if money is mentioned once again this evening.'

The front-door bell rang, long and firmly. Instantly the aunts drew together, asking, 'Who's that?' glancing at the poker handy in the grate.

'Well, isn't Gibby ever going to answer it?' said Aunt Cissie, her eyes bright.

The door opened and Gibby poked her head in.

'Who's that?' she asked.

'Don't worry, Gibby. I'll see who it is.' I got up and went out into the hall, feeling the petrified silence of the four of them at my back. Ignoring a faint cry of, 'Put the door on the chain first!' I opened it and stepped back.

It was Max.

THIRTEEN

'AM I COMING in or are you coming out?' he asked, and stepped into the hall.

It was so extraordinary to see him; to see any man not in an album, pressed flat in a photograph, that I couldn't say a word. I put out a hand. He was just the same and the overwhelming impression was of his solidity, his sanity. He was like a safe bush, jutting out from a cliff face, down which I was slipping fast. He was utterly familiar, and yet he embarrassed me. But I found that my hand was still resting on his unresponsive arm.

'You hung up on me,' he said, 'and I couldn't ring you back. I daren't ring you here, it was too late. So I came.'

'I ran out of pennies.'

My wooden face did something to him, for a small nerve under his right eye began to twitch, and his discomposure reassured and astonished me.

'Do you want to meet the aunts?' I asked, in a high hostess-gabble. 'We can go for a walk afterwards, or would you like some coffee? We've had tea.'

Looking over my shoulder he evidently spotted Gibby peering round the drawing-room door, and waved to her. She vanished into the room.

'It looks as if they rather expect me to say good evening,' he said. 'Lead on.'

As we reached the drawing-room door Gibby scuttled out of it, gave us both a tumbril grin, and made for her kitchen. He was right behind me as I went in and faced the aunts. Aunt Seraphina took in at one glance his coloured shirt, woollen tie, old sports jacket, and set her face into a making-the-best-of-it expression. Aunt Rosa appeared to withdraw two feet, although she did not move from her chair. Aunt Cissie spun her chair round and cried out:

'Well, Max at last! Made your fortune yet, my boy?'

'No,' said Max quietly. 'Have you?'

There was a spreading nervous titter from all three old ladies.

'Have you had tea?' asked Aunt Rosa, and at the same time Aunt Seraphina said, 'Such a long time; we thought you were dead.'

'Yes, thank you,' said Max, perfectly polite, in Aunt Rosa's direction and, turning slightly to Aunt Seraphina, he added, 'Well, we all seem to be alive, don't we?'

There was a pause. Aunt Cissie, who recovered quickly, asked the question they were all longing to put, but didn't quite dare.

'Have you come to take her home?'

'She seems perfectly at home here.'

'I should hope so, she was brought up here.' Aunt Seraphina bent down to put more coal on the fire, and there was another pause. He asked Aunt Cissie about her accident, but she was too inquisitive to enjoy his concern. At last he said, turning to me, where I stood, frozen, against one of the small tables, 'I have one or two things to discuss with Louie. I thought we might go for a walk over the common. It's a beautiful evening.'

'Oh, is it?' said Aunt Rosa. 'There's a terrible wind out. We haven't been across the common for years. It's changed. Wrap up warm, dear, or you'll get a chill.' She had turned to me while she spoke, and now added, 'Will you be bringing Max back to supper?'

'No, thank you,' said Max. 'I have to be in town by nine o'clock. It's kind of you, though. Slip a coat on, Lou. We haven't much time.'

I went upstairs, did my face, came down to the hall and put on a coat, then went back to fetch Max. The atmosphere had changed; they were all relaxing under his quiet, easy manner. Later, when we walked down the cut and out on to the windy common, he told me that he had set out to charm them. In the short while I had been away they had invited him to come again, and Aunt Seraphina had twinkled at him like a girl. The next day she said to me, 'I can't understand why you should want to leave that charming man. Such a gentleman, in spite of those dreadful clothes.'

'I haven't left him; I've just come on a visit to you,' I told her.

Now I said to Max, 'They don't know a thing. They think I'm on a visit.'

He did not reply, so I went on, 'I feel as if we've just met, why's that?'

'Because you've slipped back into being the daughter of the house. Doing what you're told, putting on a warm coat, slipping out on the sly to telephone. In the name of God, Louie, why? We're married, remember?'

'Max,' I said, stopping, 'I don't want a row.'

'We couldn't row. We're not close enough. All we could do if we were foolish is to bicker in a rather arid way. That's not why I came. I can't just sit at home in the flat and ask myself *why*. You'll have to tell me, and then I'll go away.'

The setting sun struck the odd protuberance my grandfather had built on to the side of the house. It was his own conservatory, and now it glowed like a false ruby. A spiral staircase of iron twisted down to the garden, and it occurred to me that it was in there he had raised the rare lily, the one he had celebrated. I made a mental note to investigate it in the morning. These things seemed more real than Max, walking beside me without touching arm or hand. He noticed the direction of my eyes.

'D'you want the house? Is that it? Could you live in a

suburb? I love this common, it's alive, it's open. . . . But that house . . . darling, what's happened to you? What are you afraid of?'

He put his arm round me at last, held my head up against his ear until I softened against him. Only then was I aware of the tension that flowed out of my body: I had been as rocklike as the aunts.

I chose to answer the last question.

'You know what I'm afraid of. The poison at the root of the family that breaks people up. Don't you realize that only the women survive, Max? Husbands die or go away; nothing ever goes right. We don't seem able to have a child. I thought that by going back I could find out what it is that makes us – closed in. A whirlpool instead of a stream. I must know what dammed up the family. And I'm beginning to find out . . . I think.'

I had spoken the last words so softly that he did not hear them. At any rate, he released me, and took my hand as we walked over the tussocky grass, towards the two ponds.

'You're inventing reasons for going back to prison. You wanted to see the last of them, but they go on and on. They make you feel guilty, being young and' – he hesitated, hating to give a word more than its precise meaning – 'in love and living your own life. You hoped you'd find them broken, but they're not. They'll break you if you can't resist them.'

He sounded like my father, so I brought out the letter. I made him sit down, even though the grass was damp and, while we smoked to keep off the midges, I told him about young Mr Bradshaw, and gave him the letter to read. Out of context the letter was mad, of course. But then all sudden things appear so. Our cigarettes glowed brighter as the light faded and the thin pages crackled under his hand as he bent to read the fine writing. I seemed condemned to read the letter by a difficult light.

113

'I wish I'd known him,' he said at last, looking thoughtfully over the mist rising from the hollows. 'All this is exactly what one senses. But what's this about suicide?'

The fact that we were several hundred pounds better off did not seem to concern him at all.

'What do you hope to find out?' he asked. 'Here's your father explaining why the aunts are like they are. Scandal, shock, pride. They've atrophied. It's simple, Louie. It's tragic, but it's happened and there's nothing you can do about it. What's your problem?'

I told him what Gibby had told me, then I said, 'I owe them something. They brought me up, after all, in that house. I sometimes think it has a bloodstream of its own. It's more than a carapace to them, unless it's one made out of their own nerves and tissues. The awful thing is, Max, that the dead in that house are not allowed to rest. That's what it is. Every single one of my aunts and uncles is still alive in each room. The aunts won't let them go. They feed on them.'

Max took my cold hands in his and looked at me calmly.

'What else? You're building up an emotional block. Tell me what is really the matter?'

So at last, after all these years, I had to tell him about the lie. It came out painfully; it was agony, tearing this truth from its hiding-place. But once told, it was the truth; and if the fact of the lie remained, then at least it was exposed. Perhaps, like all corpses, it would disintegrate in the open air.

'I thought you wouldn't wait, you see. So I had to force my grandmother's hand, and this was the only way.'

'Yes, I see,' said Max. 'So that was why she changed her mind. She didn't seem the person to do so. And that was why she never came to see us again —'

'We were abroad, don't forget, and she died soon after.'

'So we were.'

'She never told the aunts,' I said hopefully. 'But, Max, she

114

didn't *say* anything to me. She didn't blame me. She accepted it at once, as if, well, as if such a thing was inevitable. That's what I can't understand.'

Max got up and walked, quickly, nervously, to the edge of the water, and threw in his cigarette with a twirling motion. It hissed out in the silence.

'All the same it was damnable, Louie. I liked your grandmother. She was aware. She had a healthy selfishness. You chose the one thing she couldn't fight. You probably killed her.'

'Max! Max! What a vile thing to say! How dare you! I wish now I hadn't told you. She was old. She had to die some time.'

He waited until I had calmed down, then he squatted beside me.

'That had to be said once, so now it needn't ever be said again. Come on, let's walk.'

We found a path, followed it to a small railway bridge, leaned on the parapet. He began to talk, gently, not accusingly, as if solving some problem for us both.

'So that's why you're still accepting the aunts on a child's terms, not an adult's. To you they represent security, the past, a kiss for a hurt knee. You still get your own way like a sly child. It isn't good enough, Louie. And we've been building on sand, because I'm a sort of prize you won by cheating. Or the lollipop you bought with a stolen penny . . . Yes, I see why you had to come back. To grow up. It isn't them you want to expose: it's yourself. Why can't you leave them alone? Leave them to their illusions. Let them play their Game, as you call it, until they're in a rosy glow of the past. What does it matter to you? Or to us?'

A train beat its way underneath us, leaving a trail of flying sparks on the increasing darkness. As the noise thinned into an insect buzz, I said stubbornly:

'They must face reality as I do. They must know that I

know about grandfather and get it into perspective. I won't let them hide things from me. It isn't fair.'

'Isn't fair? Isn't fair? There you go again. What can you give them in place of their illusions? They can't grow up. You can. They were born in a different world, in a time when everyone had his place and nothing of value could be destroyed. We were born into a world without belief, without security; we've always known the worst and we have no illusions. At least, I haven't, and my students haven't.'

'Oh, so I'm odd man out again?' I said bitterly. 'You and your damned students. What do they do but spill their guts on to canvas? It's better to keep them hidden. It's braver to keep up a façade, like the aunts, even if it is an illusion.'

But Max had made his point. He was right as usual. And if keeping their illusions intact meant that he would not insist on my telling the aunts about the lie, then I would go along with him. He sighed, looked at his watch. We walked on, past the new tennis courts.

'The point is,' he said, lighting two cigarettes and handing one to me, 'the point is that the Braithwaites at least have the courage to go on living in their own dreams. You're only half-Braithwaite, as your father reminded you: that's why you suffer. You're half in the dream and half out. You're tugged both ways. You went back to look for two old women who'd be grateful for your interest —'

'That's not true —'

'Well, it's part of the truth. You assumed, as the young always do, that the old are much obliged, kind madam, for this crust you throw. It isn't so at all. The old are more self-sufficient than you think. If they need young people at all, its merely as a term of reference, they like them as an audience. The young can't just step in and take over the old. They must live a parallel life on their own terms; you can't thrust the old away, either, because physically they need care. No one despises a young child for being dependent, so —'

'This is a new track,' I said hatefully, 'I thought you cared only for the young.'

'I care for every human being —'

'Oh!' I cried out in despair, 'You drive me round in circles! You've always hated the aunts and all they stood for. You've been as jealous as hell every time they asked me to go home. I can't understand you —'

'Home. That's just it. Home should be with me. We're married. Sorry, that's where I came in. You haven't transferred your home yet. That's what I resent. And they make you ill.' I made to interrupt him, but he held out a hand and spoke so painfully I had to listen, although I wanted to run away from him again. 'Listen. It was my fault, all of it. The whole thing was too quick. You were like a strawberry runner broken off from the parent plant before you'd made your own roots.'

'Thanks very much.'

He nodded tiredly, as if this was what he expected. 'You were quite right to come back. You are braver than I am, because you face up to what you most fear —'

'Max, don't. Please —'

I could not bear him to lay himself open before me. He had only done this once before, many years ago; he could only do so with someone he trusted entirely. And this responsibility was more dreadful than anything I might find the aunts had done or had not done, or had been done to them. From that moment on, the past ceased to be as important as the present, and it was the first strengthening thought that had come to me for months. That something good and new might come out of the present had not occurred to me. But this could only be handled by not being handled.

'Oh,' I said casually, taking Max's hand, 'we look for our heroes in the wrong places. We make too much of things. Think of Valery's poem we read:

Les derniers dons, et les doigts qui les défendent,
Tout va sous terre et rentrent dans le jeu.

'Yes,' said Max. 'We don't seem able to escape the game, do we?'

'Max,' I asked suddenly, shivering against the chill of the night, 'since this is freedom-of-speech day, what is it *you* most fear?'

'Loss of personal identity. Without that, relationships have no point. Come on, we'd better get you back before they call the police.'

We stopped by the cut, but I did not want to be left there, so he took me round to the front gate, and there we stood by the holly hedge like an absurd courting couple, reluctant to say good night.

'Max, give me a week or two.'

He kissed me. 'All right. You're in the past, and I can't follow you there. But listen, darling, I'm in the present, and I love you and I want you to get unstuck. You must do it yourself or it won't be any good.' He walked away, then came back to where I was still waiting. 'Oh, and we'll have a child, even if we have to conceive it on the common. I'm sure of it. And it won't be the first to be gotten that way.'

Leaning against the gatepost, I suddenly shook with laughter, and down the road Max turned, waved, and was gone.

FOURTEEN

'Well,' said Gibby the next morning, 'fancy him coming and me never gettin' a word with him. I always liked him; you know that. You could have brought him out to the kitchen, Miss Lou.'

'He didn't stay long.'

I was helping her with the vegetables, peeling potatoes at the sink. Max's unexpected arrival had stirred the house into a fury of speculation, and it was to escape the aunts' questions that I had come out here. I was especially annoyed with Aunt Rosa, who had said quietly, 'I hope you didn't tell him about the money, dear. Otherwise you'll never know where you stand.'

I had made some sharp retort and left her, and she had retired to her room with a headache, although it was her afternoon for visiting Miss Protheroe and her brother.

'Will he be coming again?' asked Gibby. 'Whatever *they* say, *I* think he's a good sort. Simple. Not like my Nige; sharp as a needle is Nige. Did I tell you he was coming to see me tomorrow? Suddenly remembered he's got a mother. Must want something.' She smiled proudly, as if Nigel's neglect made him even sharper. 'Might bring his youngest, if his wife'll let him.'

'Why shouldn't she?' I was anxious to get off the subject of Max, in whose arrival I could scarcely believe, apart from a new feeling of well-being and relaxation.

Gibby gave her barking chuckle, and started to beat up eggs for the custard. '*She* says she's married beneath her, doesn't like her mother-in-law to be in service. Ho no. Too uppity by half, is Miss Iris Higgs. As if being in Woolworth's behind the scent counter put her above *me*!'

She added milk and a bayleaf, turned the mixture into a double saucepan and stirred it carefully, measuring in sugar. 'I'll tell you something, Miss Lou. Nige is coming to get me to go and live with them, that's what. So that my lady can go out to work again and leave me to look after the kids. Kids! As if I haven't had enough, and her with a kitchen half the size of this scullery. Those council houses are built with newspaper and spit I always say. Noise! You should hear it. I swear you can hear a man gargling five houses away. . . .'

My stomach retched uncomfortably. I couldn't imagine Gibby gone. Selfishly I thought, 'Who will look after the aunts if she does go?' and remembered a remark of Max's as we walked home the previous evening. Gibby made sense of the house, he had said. She was real. She bolstered up the aunts, protecting them from the world as it was, stretching strong as a chain back into their mother's time.

'But, Gibby, I never think of you being in service here. You're part of the family. I can't think of this place without you. Oh! You wouldn't go, would you?'

My anxiety, which made me cut myself deeply with the sharp potato knife, pleased her. All the same, it reminded her that she had a choice. I swear that, because of my ill-considered words, a tiny sense of power entered her mind for the first time. She said teasingly, as she bound up my finger with a clean handkerchief:

'Well, I'm getting on, Miss Lou. And the kids are my grandchildren. I've thought once or twice lately that this house is a bit much for all of us. And what about me if my two ladies listen to Miss Cissie's nonsense about living in an hotel? I'll be on the streets then, with only my pension book to cover me at nights.'

It was then I decided that I would contrive to be there when Nigel came. I laughed away the idea of my aunts moving to an hotel; said that Aunt Cissie was full of ideas. It was more than probable that she would move in here. Another mistake. Gibby frowned.

'She'd take some looking after, that one.' Cunningly, she tried blackmail. 'Now if you and your hubby moved in, that'd be different. We'd have a man about the house at last. Young blood. And you never know, Miss Lou: next time you may be lucky. You want a proper home for a child, and wouldn't they be pleased, those two!' She took up the knife and went on with the potatoes. 'Put the kettle on, dearie, and let's have a quiet cup of tea. It's always a shock, losing blood. You've gone pale.'

I did what I was told, and she said, looking into the murky water among the potato skins as if she were a seer, 'You didn't rest up enough. Young women today don't put their feet up when they're expecting. They rush about and go on drinking and smoking – and *you* smoke too much, if you don't mind my mentionin' it, with your chest – and then wonder why the baby can't stay put. You shake it about so, poor little mite. How long did you go?'

'Both times, three months.'

Gibby shook her head. 'My sister had to lay up from the first month. Eight months in bed she was and weak as a kitten when she got up. Then the milk flew to her legs and she was never the same after.'

'Did she have the baby?'

'Ten-pounder it was and like a bladder of lard. Pale! Lardy I called him and lardy he was 'till he was took with pneumonia when he was five. Then she had twins, and jumping about all the time she was carrying. They were born on a bus. We had to laugh. So you see you never can tell what's for the best.'

'Well,' I said, bemused, 'it all seems to be a matter of luck.'

'Kettle's boilin',' she said, giving one of her half grunts, 'Luck! Don't talk to me about luck in this family.'

Aunt Seraphina came in from the garden as I made the tea. It was not one of her good days, no illusion held for her; an early frost had punished her dahlias and age had stamped itself in wrinkles on her face. She stood by the kitchen window in her heavy Blücher boots, a wartime bargain, her old tweed coat, and drank her tea, looking out into the sodden garden.

'That garden looks as I feel, finished,' she complained. 'The damp's got into my back again. Oh, I never thought I'd dread the winter, Louie. That's what it is to be old. I wanted to die young, you know, to —'

'Ssh, ssh!' scolded Gibby, from the scullery, 'that's no way to talk. Die young indeed, whatever next!'

But I knew what my aunt meant. Her life could not contain her dreams. She had wanted to die beautifully, to be mourned, an opera singer in embryo. 'The sudden death of the talented Miss Seraphina Braithwaite will be deplored by all lovers of the opera. . . .' 'A Jenny Lind nipped in the bud . . .' 'It would not be rash to say that in the early passing of this young singer we have lost another divine Melba. . . .'

And looking at her peevish face in the cold light of the window I remembered another, very different, dream; one she had told me about. A huntsman, she had said, was calling his pack over the hills, and first of all they were far away; she could not hear the voices of the hounds as she wandered about the valley, uprooting rare flowers for her garden. Then, as she grew older, the dream changed. She saw herself going more slowly, and each time she dreamed it, the huntsman's horn sounded nearer, and she heard the voices of the leading hounds. Today, I saw with pity that the hunt was closing in.

So, to make amends for still being young, for having Max (for I was sure that it was his visit as well as Aunt Cissie's arrival which had upset her), I said that I would massage her back with grandmother's special ointment. But she was not entirely appeased. She sat down and pulled off one of her heavy boots and looked dispiritedly at her foot. I knelt down and pulled off the other. Then I took both feet in my hands and looked closely at the toes that showed beneath the lisle stockings.

'Aunt Seraphina, you have a corn!'

I was truly shocked, for I had never seen either of my aunts or my grandmother with any kind of blemish on their feet. They had always been very much concerned with their personal appearance. It went with the rigid framework that had encompassed their upbringing. The image was the thing; the overall image built up by habit and discipline. The aunts, under my grandmother's tutelage, had taken care to preserve, within the larger moral framework of their lives, and within the physical framework of the actual running of a house and family, yet another, more exacting discipline: absolute cleanliness of person and dress at all times. It did not matter if no one saw them: they must always be immaculate; it was a matter of principle. But my grandmother went even further. There was an invisible judge, she used to say; we were watched at all times. Not the merest feather on a sparrow went uncounted.

Whether she expected this invisible judge to materialize one day on the doorstep of The Hollies and demand an immediate inspection, I never dared to ask. But if he did, the occupants were ready. Hair, hands, feet, skin, teeth: all were scrupulously cared for by every means within their power. For years we cleaned our teeth with crushed cooking-salt mixed with camphorated chalk, enlivened by a squeeze of lemon: I remember the guilty joy with which I bought my first tube of toothpaste when I went away to school.

My grandmother was a great one for home-made remedies: rosewater and glycerin for the hands; almond oil, olive oil and lemon juice for nearly everything. She washed her beautiful hair with green Castile soap and egg-yolks and rosemary. My aunts never used soap on their faces, only a cleansing cream and lotions they made up themselves. All the Braithwaite women had fine skins, yielding and pink as the suède backing to their swansdown puffs. But my grandmother's true fanaticism was kept for feet. A chiropodist visited the house once a fortnight to pare away hard skin and look out for fallen arches. Fallen arches she feared more than the blindness that came on her in her sixties. I remember quite clearly, as a small child, furiously resenting having to wear buttoned boots at home. 'To support your ankles and preserve your arches,' said my grandmother, 'see how pretty they look!' And she would herself kneel before me as I sat glumly in the big chair while she twinkled away with a button-hook.

As I grew older, I was called on to do the delicate and intimate things for my grandmother and aunts that in a wealthier household would have been done by a lady's maid. I pulled the odd, sprouting hairs on their chins, massaged their feet with warm olive oil to keep away chilblains – and, as my grandmother's sight failed, trimmed her fingernails, and toenails, too, in between Mr Partridge's visits.

I shall never quite forget the smell of her very clean, well-shaped white feet. She had straight toes and pretty, rounded nails; there was no hard skin anywhere and not a sign of a vein on her smooth legs. But it was then that I learned that feet had an aura of their own: they were far more characteristic than hands, and the curious enclosed smell that came from them was more than I could bear. It was like opening a box that had been shut for years; there is a dark secret whiff about the tiny puff of escaping air. I hated this scarcely perceptible smell of feet on my hands after I had put the scissors away and would wash repeatedly as I watched grandmother slowly feeling round the toes in search of the slightest roughness. We would then dust them over with a mixture of powdered orris root and chalk. . . .

So now, holding my aunt's foot, seeing the hard circle on her little toe, I was horrified.

'Don't you have anyone come to do your feet?'

'Mr Partridge died years ago,' replied Aunt Seraphina with her bitter, deprived little smile. 'His daughter took over the practice, but she hadn't the same touch, not the same touch at all. Quite rough – oh, a terrible person! Once she actually cut into my flesh and made it bleed. "Don't do that, oh don't do that, you're hurting!" I told her. And she said, gripping my foot quite hard, "It's your fault, Miss Braithwaite. You moved your toe." What mama would have said I don't know. So of course we stopped her coming.'

'Well, I won't hurt you; don't worry.'

'Ah,' she said unexpectedly, her face smooth again, 'you're a good girl. You were always gentle.' Experimentally she felt round her chin. 'Now do you remember you used to pull out these hairs for me? There's a small mole, only a very small one, and a very fine hair . . . ah, here it is. Now, if you'll just run to my room and bring down the little tweezers in the top lefthand drawer . . .'

When I came down she still had her finger on her chin.

'Yes, here it is, Louie. Careful now; I'll turn to the light. Take a firm hold, dear, and pull. Ah! you've got it. Let me see.' Together we examined the fine black hair, and made sure the root was out as well. 'Splendid. It's been worrying me for days.'

She was much happier now. She loved being the centre of attention. Guiltily I realized how little it took to make her happy. Then, typically, she remarked with irrelevance, 'I wonder what Cissie's feet are like? Have you seen them yet?'

'Why, yes,' I replied. 'I helped her into her caliper this

morning. Oh, Aunt Seraphina, her leg's so thin, it's terrible. I can't think she'll ever walk again.'

'She'll never be out of that chair,' Aunt Seraphina agreed unconcernedly. 'But what about her feet?'

I realized that she was jealous, so I told her that they looked all right to me. I would attend to them for her.

'Someone's been doing them, then, all this time. Harry left her very well off, dear; he had plenty of money. Still, *I* wouldn't have had him if he'd been studded with diamonds. Ah yes. Money talks.' But she was losing interest. 'I wonder what she's up to now?' she said.

She did not have to wait long. There was a battering noise at the kitchen door and I went over and opened it. Aunt Cissie sat outside in her wheelchair; at once she came speeding in.

'Cups of tea at all hours!' she exclaimed. 'Ah, now I know I'm home! Louie, I wonder if you'd take me round to see the Protheroes this afternoon? Rosa isn't up to it; she's not up to it at all. One of her bad heads. Something seems to have upset her.'

She shot me a sharp look, but I did not rise to it. I had placated one aunt and did not feel like exerting myself again.

'Yes, of course I'll take you,' I said. 'I haven't seen the Protheroes for years. I don't expect they'll remember me. Aunt Rosa is wise to lie down if she has a headache.'

With which I hurried out of the kitchen, on the excuse of tidying up my tidy, scarcely disturbed room.

FIFTEEN

'WE'LL GIVE THEM such a surprise,' said Aunt Cissie, tapping her hands on the arms of her wheelchair. 'I haven't seen old Bill Protheroe for ten years. He came to Harry's funeral. Looked most distinguished. Rosa says he's senile, and that Lucy's memory is going. Well, we'll soon see. That front garden needs weeding. Gives a bad impression.'

We were bowling along Chestnut Crescent, where the houses were less impressive than The Hollies. They had been built later and were semi-detached. The aunts often said that once there had been fields, just fields, stretching for miles. 'It was a gentleman's park, with fine old chestnut trees, but builders got hold of it.' I knew my grandfather had held shares in this company, but my aunts preferred to forget the fact. The houses had ugly jutting bow fronts, half stucco, half brick and, instead of a semi-circle of drive, a short path led up to the deep porches. In the Protheroes' front garden stood a faded-looking gnome, fishing in a cement pond.

Aunt Cissie stopped the wheelchair as I pushed her through the gate. She swung her arm dramatically towards the gnome.

'Throw it out, Louie! Go on – throw it out! Lowers the district, that sort of thing. One expects it on housing estates, for that kind of person knows no better. Lucy must be out of her mind.'

Luckily, before I could make a move, or remonstrate, the front door opened, and a fat little white-haired woman stood on the doorstep. She wore a matching grey cardigan and skirt, with a frilly white blouse. Food stains edged the frill, and her vague brown eyes wandered over us.

'Miss Protheroe, I've brought my aunt to see you. Aunt Rosa —'

'They've telephoned. They've spoken to me on the telephone. Yes. One of her migraines. Poor Rosa. Oh, but Cissie, my poor girl, how are you? Do come in. Can I help. No, perhaps I'd better not. . . .'

She teetered on the doorstep, which was very clean, much cleaner than her person, blocking the way. She appeared to be thrown into a confusion of words and indecision.

'Lucy, I'm delighted to see you. That gnome, though —'

'You like him? He's my good-luck pixie: we found him in Cornwall. I call him Mr Hopeful because there aren't any fish in the pond!'

She opened her little mouth and seemed to gargle at us.

Aunt Cissie whispered to me as I eased the chair up the step:

'Rosa's mistaken. This is the one who's senile. But then she always was a fool.' Raising her voice pleasantly, she asked about Bill.

'He's in the drawing-room, looking forward to the treat. It *is* a treat, after all these years. He's had his nap and now he's quite lively. Yes, quite lively. Now, isn't this nice? Such a surprise. Yes. Shall I take your hat?'

'No thank you,' said Aunt Cissie, disapprovingly. 'One keeps one's hat on for tea.'

We were in the drawing-room now and I saw that the net curtains darkened what little light came through fairly heavily leaded windows.

'Still putting people in their place, Cissie,' said an old man's voice from a deep chair by the window. He rose and dwarfed us all. Extreme height, extreme emaciation, set him apart from us. He leaned on a thick, silver-knobbed stick and waited.

I hadn't seen Mr Protheroe for years, and yet now he seemed sharply familiar. There was something about the way he moved, the stiffness, the height . . . it might have been the photographs we had been looking at, of course. I knew he had gone off to India to a tea plantation after his disappointment in love, and nothing had been heard of him for twenty years. Now he had come home, retired, to live with his sister. He was greeting Aunt Cissie in an old man's humming voice, as if some vital spring had snapped.

'Never thought to see you tethered to a chair, eh, eh?' He bent and clasped her vital little hands in his long biscuit-coloured ones. His nails, I noticed, were very flat and square and unused looking. At once I remembered something else about him, something I could say when he turned to me.

'And I never expected to see you, Willie Protheroe, living in a house with a gnome in the garden. Dear God, what's happened to us all?'

But he was already turning, like an antique clockwork man, to me, and I realized that he must have some trouble with his back, and also that, having thought out a sentence, he expelled it like an arrow and never troubled to see where it landed. He might never have heard Aunt Cissie's rejoinder. While his sister made sprightly, almost flirtatious conversation about the gnome, 'Oh, my poor Mr Hopeful, how can you be so unkind to him?' Mr Protheroe bent his head from his high shoulders and gave me a long look.

'Mary's girl, isn't it? Your mother just missed being a beauty, Lou – Louise, isn't it? Yes. Thought I'd forgotten, didn't you? I remember you when you were —' He put out a trembling hand three feet from the floor, looking at me all the time with his big, pale blue pupils that swam in their liquid containers like trapped fish.

'Do you remember a long time ago teaching me how to weed your lawn, Mr Protheroe?' I asked him now, speaking slowly and encouragingly. I wanted to catch his attention fully before the walking mechanism slowed and he sank back into the shadows of his chair. 'You told me to push my nail under the creeping bits of clover and then pull, rather than pick off the leaves.' I could see him now, creeping on all fours over his small lawn, sliding one of those broad, flat nails beneath a clover tendril and easing it up with a crow of triumph.

He pushed out his lower lip, which was broad and lax, like a piece of overwashed elastic and almost as pale, and shook his head.

'I remember you stirring up my fish. You were a naughty little girl. One died.'

At once an unfairness that had lain uneasy and forgotten for many years stung me with a child's sharp sense of injustice. I said, more violently than was permissible, 'You never believed me. I didn't stir up the fish. I put in a stick to lift out a frog.'

'Ah, ah!' crowed the old man, wiping his watering eyes with a large clean handkerchief. 'You've still got a conscience after all these years! Why did the fish die, then?'

'I don't know,' I said wretchedly. The child vanished after making a reproachful face. What was the good of growing up, she seemed to say as she edged through the French windows into the garden, if you can't clear up even a little thing like this?

'There now, don't quarrel, you two, when you haven't met for years,' scolded Miss Protheroe. 'I'm going to bring in the tea. Will you help me, my dear? The trolley catches on the edge of the carpet and spills the milk.' As we went out of the door together, she turned to her brother and said distinctly, 'And you know perfectly well, Bill, it was Seraphina who stirred your fish. She was in a temper about something, I remember distinctly . . . but of course Fina could do no wrong.' She closed the door behind her quite loudly.

In the kitchen I took her by the arm.

130

'Miss Protheroe, are you sure? Everyone was so cross at the time. Why ever didn't Aunt Seraphina —'

'I can't remember any more, my dear. Only that Fina was in a paddy. Willie was a great one for teasing in those days, and I saw her stirring up the fish and when you'd all gone home one floated up, white. I told him. But no, he was sweet on her, you see. I thought it was spiteful, stirring —'

I had heard enough. It was like the Game. A truth, a half-truth, a downright lie; they overlaid each other like petals in a pot pourri, vital oils gone, uniformly brown. I looked out into the garden and saw, hanging from a line in the concealed backyard that hid dustbins and the outside lavatory and a shed of sorts, several old people's dispirited garments: long-legged knickers, pink; long underpants, wool. They hung in the heavy moist air with drying-up cloths and dusters and depressed me. I felt hemmed in by the old; by their faulty memories, their failing bodies. The house, in spite of its cleanliness, had a smell of old age which was missing from The Hollies.

'We'll have China tea,' Miss Protheroe was saying, 'it might take Willie's mind off India. Now, where has Mrs Roberts put it? She said she'd left everything ready. China tea, China tea, where are you?'

It was rather gruesome watching Miss Protheroe peer about, playing hide-and-seek with the tea, so I looked quickly around me and picked up a square tin with a dragon on the lid, which had been put ready by the teapot. Obviously the absent Mrs Roberts knew her employer. The cleanliness of the doorstep and this kitchen paid her tribute.

'Warm the pot, then, warm the pot. Little pot, you must be hot,' sang Miss Protheroe, while she rinsed the teapot. 'The kettle's just breathing; turn the gas up, dear. The water must be on the boil and you take the pot to the kettle. Pot to kettle, not kettle to pot, or tea won't be good, and it won't be hot. My dear mother taught me that and I've never forgotten it. You'll go a long way if you can make a good cup of tea, she used to say.' All at once she looked lost, as if wondering whether the destination was worth the travel. But she cheered up again as I complimented her on her memory, and together we edged along the hall and into the drawing-room, where Aunt Cissie was talking in a lively manner. Her words fell in a reviving shower on Mr Protheroe, who sat slumped back in his chair, his eyes fixed on her face.

'Of course,' she was saying, 'they want me to come back and live with them. But would you believe it, Bill, they haven't got a television. I'm having one put in my room, of course, while I'm there. I'm in dada's study. You remember dada, don't you, Bill?'

Did he mind sometimes being addressed as Bill and at other times as Willie? Apparently not, and for his sister and my aunt the two names seemed interchangeable. For myself, Willie suited him better, with those floating pale eyes; but I could imagine him in the past, fooling around as Bill. 'Bill's such a clown!' I could hear them say it, giggling over their croquet.

'I remember the party he gave. Champagne all the way. Pink champagne. We drank it all night watching that 'straordinary flower. Thought it'd never stop blooming. 'Straordinary. 'Straordinary chap, your father.' It was a long sentence for him, and his eyes steadied as he spoke.

I was handing him his cup, and I said, quickly, 'The *Keng hua*? The famous lily? The Chinese lily? It blooms all night, doesn't it, until dawn. Aunt Seraphina told me. What a marvellous sight it must have been.'

'That was a long time ago, Willie. We've forgotten all that, haven't we, Lucy?' said Aunt Cissie, sharp as a knife. 'China tea, how delicious. Yes, please, and one of your scones. Mrs Roberts still with you? We've still got poor old Gibby, as you know. Really, she —'

'I haven't forgotten,' said Mr Protheroe. 'I remember the past. The further back a thing is, the clearer. Couldn't tell you what I had for dinner yesterday, though. Not worth it, ha, ha.' He leant forward to me and went on quickly, as if afraid of being interrupted. 'Things happened to us, young lady, oh yes. Now that party. Something happened after that party. Caused quite a stir, quite a stir. Oh my word, yes . . .'

'We were children,' said Aunt Cissie, with entreaty. 'We were young. We can't remember things clearly.'

'*I* wasn't a child,' said Mr Protheroe obstinately. His cup rattled in his old hand. 'I'm older than you, Cissie. I expect you were sent to bed.'

'You were in the picture, Mr Protheroe. The picture they took, the flashlight one! You were all holding your glasses up, toasting the lily. How exciting it must have been. . . .' I stopped, looked at him. He was also, I realized without doubt, the man on the common who had been watching me that other morning. Full of inexplicable unease, I glanced at my aunt. On her face was the slow unrolling of a remembered nightmare. Miss Protheroe merely looked bewildered, but interested. Our excitement animated her.

'If I hadn't got up late for my morning walk, I'd have been the one to find the girl, not your gardener fellow, Cissie.' An old grudge stirred, parted muddy waters; the pale lips, pressed together, were licked, opened. 'Always take a constitutional before breakfast, wakes up the liver. Across the common, round the ponds and up through that cut, like clockwork. But we didn't get to bed before dawn that morning. Must've have been four o'clock. What a party that was!'

None of us said anything. I was too afraid of sending this fugitive memory scurrying back into unbeatable thickets, and the other two were held as if by a story, old, yet new in the telling.

'Shocking tragedy! Haven't thought about it for years. The mind's a funny thing: can't remember what I had for dinner yesterday, but I can see that crowd round your garden gate as clearly as I see you. Staring in from the common like fools. Just caught a glimpse of her face before the bobby covered it. Common little face, but young. My age, I reckoned. Horrible thing was this slug made a trail right across her cheek. Made her look like a dead branch, or a dead rabbit. And her boots shone, too. Must've been there quite a time – the dew, y'know. Party broke up at dawn, we didn't hear a thing.' He looked at us over his cold tea, 'Seems like yesterday.'

Aunt Cissie spoke after a long pause, in a voice unlike her own.

'Dada had the gate bolted after that, people used to stare so. Oh, how we hated the common after that!'

'Who was she?'

Unexpectedly, Miss Protheroe answered me, 'A servant girl from the next road. Foolish of her to be out so late, on the common, too. A lot of people lost their maids after that. They wouldn't stay, said there was a maniac around.'

'Was the man caught?'

'Caught?' Old Mr Protheroe had sucked the subject dry; now he wanted his tea. 'Pour this away, Lucy, and give me a hot cup. And let's try one of Mrs Roberts's scones. Yes, plenty of strawberry jam. That's right.' He stuffed a whole scone into his mouth and jerked his jaws until it was all swallowed. 'No, he was never caught. Scared off, I s'pose, by the police swarming all over the place. They pulled in the usual sort of scoundrels for questioning – tramps and so on, who slept in the bushes.'

'He'd be caught today,' said Miss Protheroe. 'They're cleverer today.'

'Why choose *our* garden?' asked Aunt Cissie out of an outraged past. 'Why ruin *us*?'

I thought a moment.

'Maybe the girl tried to run in through the gate. It's an iron-barred one you can slip your hand through. The others in the other gardens are mostly wooden, with bolts.'

'The gate was open,' said old Mr Protheroe. 'She was half in and half out, and her clothes —'

'That's enough,' said my aunt briskly. 'Let's not sup on horrors, Willie. I'm amazed you should have remembered it so clearly after all these years.'

'I've never thought about it until today,' he said.

Then why, I wanted to ask him, why walk on the common at dawn and look at the garden, and shake your stick at a woman sitting on the wall? It must have given him a shock, that morning, I thought, remembering him making off so stiffly for the trees.

'You weren't such a child, Cissie,' he said suddenly. 'You must have been about fifteen or thereabouts.'

'Thereabouts. Girls *were* children much longer in those days. We were tenderly reared.'

'And yet Gibby came to work for you when she was fourteen —'

'Now you're talking like a Socialist, Louie,' said my aunt. 'May I try some of that sponge, Lucy? We've been so busy talking we've forgotten our tea.'

'Slip out and put the kettle on again, dear. We'll make a fresh pot,' said Miss Protheroe to me. 'Dear me, what excitements. How lucky it wasn't one of your own servants, Cissie. There would have been talk then.'

I was half-way to the door, and looked round at this remark. My aunt's face was closed, and the silence was so absolute that I went through the door with relief, leaving the unspeakable past with them.

·　　·　　·　　·　　·

The sun was setting as we left the Protheroes' house, and Aunt Cissie was tired. She sat in her chair with a rug tucked round her and said nothing until we reached the end of the Crescent. Then suddenly she asked if I would take her along the edge of the common, so that we could come up by the cut.

The common looked beautiful under the last glow of sunlight. The sky was red and pink and blue above the turning tops of the trees and the grass shone like a pale stretch of water. The new housing estate was hidden and the illusion of being in the country was complete. Very soon the quiet mistiness of the suburbs, which I had forgotten, would swamp the roads and bushes and lie damply around the houses. A few schoolchildren loitered home, their satchels flung over their shoulders, desultorily searching for blackberries. It was too early for office workers, but later on the spiky heels of the girls would come tapping along the asphalt paths from the station; they would hurry from lamp-post to lamp-post, making the most of the pools of light that spread from the inverted glass globes, flowering in the darkness.

What sort of weather had it been, I wondered, when that little servant girl had been attacked and chased, caught and murdered?

'Nobody will attack *us*,' said my aunt, as if she had read my mind. 'By the way, Louise, don't mention anything at home. I can't imagine why Bill Protheroe wanted to bring all that up after such a long time. Lives in the past, I suppose. We all come to it.'

We were passing along the backs of the gardens, and grandfather's conservatory blazed like a beacon through the tall trees. We skirted the ditch with the nettles, passed the locked gate of The Hollies.

'Do you know why your grandfather built that thing up there?' asked my aunt, with a bark of laughter.

'Why, to catch the sun for his flowers.'

'Catch the sun. Oh yes. And other things. It was the only place where he could get away from mama. She disliked a man to smoke in the house. He was furious when she had the door made, leading through from the landing, but she had her way: mama was a determined woman. It's blocked up now, I expect. We often wondered what he found to do in there, all those hours. Stop a minute.'

We stopped by the cut and stood under the chestnut tree that leaned over the wall from the vicarage garden. The old bricks were still warm to my hand, and the last of the sun flowed palely down through the crisping leaves. Vitality being withdrawn to the source, leaving a mere map of veins which would detach easily, without pain, in the first autumn gale. If only all old age could be so calm, so that at the end the spirit merely drifted away from the body without fuss! I wondered whether Aunt Cissie or any of the aunts feared death, but it was not a question I cared to put. If I were old, I thought, I should like to die in autumn. It is a gloriously sacramental, as well as a sacrificial, season; pyres of leaves, grapes pressed for wine, corn gathered for bread. Bread and wine and Abraham's burnt offering. The end and the beginning . . . now it is autumn·and the burning leaves, and the long, long journey towards oblivion . . . But among the mellowness and the melancholy there was also violence, for no season is without it. At my feet were the broken-open husks of horse-chestnuts lying on the cold grassblades, their pale suède pockets rifled. I bent down to see whether a chestnut had been overlooked, and was lucky. A perfect nut, evidently rejected by the searching boys as too small, fitted into the palm of my hand as snugly as one of those pieces of jade the Japanese carve to fondle and bring harmony to the spirit. The nut looked like a mahogany pebble, lying there. Grown in secret darkness, protected like a jewel fit for the year's crown, it still held a polish and a depth and a perfection that I knew would soon fade. Violated, the glow would vanish, as if virtue was taken from it by too much handling, too many fond looks. . . .

Aloud, I said:

> 'Where's the cheek that doth not fade,
> Too much gazed at?'

'What's that?' My aunt opened her eyes with a jerk. I had surprised her out of a catnap, and she was ruffled. 'Where are we? Oh yes, the sun is still quite warm, I had to close my eyes against it. Now why did I ask you to bring me this way? I wanted to talk to you, that was it. I wanted – yes – you may think I'm a nosy old woman, Louie, but I can't see you flopping about here all day, when —'

Fondling the nut in my palm, passing it from one hand to the other, I watched her with a curious detachment. She must have been offended, for she suddenly lost her confused, edgy way of speaking and said straight out:

'I just wanted to ask you, Louie, why you haven't had any children. You're young, you're strong, you have a decent sort of husband even if he can't make any money. What you're doing living here with us when you should be with him I can't understand.' Her voice grew fretful, and she tried to turn in her chair to face me, but failed. Instead, she beat her hands on the arms. 'And don't tell me it's none of my business. Everything that happens in this family is my business. Your business, too. We stick together, my girl, and blood is thicker than water. You broke my mother's heart when you went off with that man, and Fina took years to get over it. She was more than a mother to you.'

It was easy, with practice, to pick out the irrelevancies in her talk and ignore the barbs. I had picked up the family habit of answering one question with another, so now I said, leaning on the back of the chair. 'If the family's business is my business, Aunt Cissie, why didn't anyone tell me that grandfather shot himself out on the common just back there?'

Aunt Cissie said nothing at all, and I pushed the chair past the cut, thinking it was impossible to go into the house, talking as we were.

'Who told you?' she said at last. 'It's getting cold, I want to go home. The sun's gone in. Which one of them told you?'

'Neither. But it doesn't matter. I know, that's all. And I can't see why you had to hush it all up. People commit suicide every day. Seven thousand people did in London alone last year. I —'

'Don't talk nonsense! People are different today. Mama thought it a sin to take life. Anyway, it's a lie, whatever you heard. Papa had an accident. He was terribly upset about that other dreadful thing – it quite spoilt his party, and he seemed to lose all interest in his flowers. He was out having some target practice when it happened and anyone who tells you differently is a liar. Your grandfather was a very sensitive man, Louie.'

I turned the chair round and we started back. The sun had gone behind the trees, throwing them into a green-gold relief, and a grey mist came creeping over the rough grass. My aunt could not keep quiet, she moved restlessly and said in her most edged tone, 'I can't understand why a girl of your age wants to live in the past. It isn't healthy. You should be busy with a family of your own, not listening to a lot of old women. I've been married twice and I know.' We went up the cut and out into the broad, safe road. 'And what's more, you're letting yourself go. There's a ladder in your stocking, I noticed it at the Protheroes. It would serve you right,' she added with relish, 'if that husband of yours left you. He's too soft.'

A charge of emotion ran like electricity down my body and through each leg to the ground, fastening me there.

'Max would never leave me,' I said thinly, dryly. 'Max and I, we —'

'He's only a man, child, not a saint, and you can try even a saint too far. What's the matter with you? Come on, I'm cold.'

With a huge effort of will I managed to move my legs. I had never before experienced such an acute physical reaction; never, even in a dream, or during an attack, had I felt such cold terror. To be alone, and alone because of someone else's action, not mine, seemed so terrible that had I not been leaning on the handles of the wheelchair I would have dissolved as the safe world around me dissolved and shifted. Later I was to realize that this was a true moment of growth, a moment when one's prejudices thinned, one's horizons widened and certain words like *death, loss, love* rang through one's consciousness with the exact melancholy of bells tolling under deep water.

I pushed her slowly up the drive, for the first time seeing myself as others saw me: immature, idiotic, neurotically barren; still the priggish over-cared-for child. Before Gibby answered our ring, my aunt said, in a quite different voice, 'Best not to rake up all that nonsense of old Bill Protheroe's again. It would only upset them. No. Let the past lie.' I did not respond, and she added fretfully, 'Louie, do you hear me? You're like a zombie, child. Now did you notice if they had a television? I quite forgot to ask. If mine doesn't come soon I'll have to go round and look in with them. At least one wouldn't have to talk.'

Gibby opened the door and helped me up the step with the chair. Once in the hall Aunt Cissie said, 'I can take myself to my room, thank you,' and shot off along the passage at speed, evidently annoyed.

'She should have a bell on that thing,' said Gibby. 'It's a danger, the way she goes. Like a devil.' Sharply she looked up into my face. 'What's the matter, then?'

'Nothing.'

However, she waited whilst I took off my hat and coat, so I was forced to add, unwillingly, 'We came back by the common. I think she must be overtired. The Protheroes were talking about – the past.'

'The ideas she gets in her head! Back by the common, indeed, and at this time of night! Let's hope she doesn't go upsetting the others. Let the past lie, I say.'

She went off to her kitchen, talking to herself, her tongue slipping effortlessly over well-worn phrases, consoling words, as the quick fingers of a Catholic woman slip over her beads, telling them for comfort.

I was perfectly willing to let the past lie. It lay now, with murder and suicide, two cold frogs, at the bottom of my mind. Only it was the future that for the first time began to engage me; it would have to be thought about in the long evening ahead. I stood alone in the hall with the slow passing of time and envied my aunts, for each of them had a private occupation into which they could retreat. I had only my own thoughts to step into, and they inhabited a cold, dis-ordered room.

SIXTEEN

I WENT UPSTAIRS at last and sat on my bed, refusing to take refuge in an attack of asthma. Max used to say that these attacks were only a way of avoiding facing up to a crisis, but I had never really believed him; he was full of odd ideas. I suppose I only picked out what I wanted to believe, as most people do, and when he told me that I suffered because I had been brought up to be rigid and the conflict came when I tried to be fluid, I accepted this explanation as I had accepted all my life the excuses people made for me.

I had to focus my attention on something, as Aunt Cissie's words ran coldly through my mind, so I looked at the picture of the two children. There they sat on their bed, clinging together, looking down at a mouse on the floor. 'What is the good of a Perfect Day, If you can't have a Perfect Night?' It filled me with exasperation, why couldn't those stupid-looking children accept the fact that mice existed, had every right to exist? Instead of crouching together there, why didn't they throw something at the mouse, stuff cotton-wool in their ears, get into bed and forget it?

But if they couldn't, how could I?

It had never occurred to me that Max might leave *me*, and this discovery of a wide area of *naïveté* within my own consciousness was utterly humiliating. Had it occurred to Max? Would I ever know? I felt like a healthy person, smug and safe, who discovers that he has in fact been for years eaten away by an internal cancer and has only a few weeks to live. That the truth should have come, like a careless arrow, from Aunt Cissie, was another shock, and the fact that there was, in this house, another person with perception, judging me, whereas I had supposed myself to be the only judge, was the second hardest thing to face.

Looking back on the last few weeks, seeing again my puny ferretings into the past, I was ashamed. I had succeeded, however clumsily, in cutting open that ripe Victoria plum of family life and finding the maggot. But as it crawled out it seemed, like all maggots, too defenceless and blind to be afraid of. One shuddered and crushed it and forgot.

Now I knew I wanted to go away from this house, back to Max. But this could not be done until every trace of dependence and weakness and humiliation had been got rid of. I must go back to Max a better person, a fuller woman. . . . But not quite yet. The first thing to accept was that now there was nowhere to run. Here I sat on my bed at The Hollies, and it was just a house, with three old women in it: my aunts. It was just a house and one could come and go as one pleased. I would go when my stature was sufficiently patched up and increased, so that, together, Max and I might achieve—what? A phrase, a tag, teased my mind, and I wondered where I had come across it, 'new kind of inter-dependence in marriage . . . two human beings loving one another and not desiring to dominate or possess . . .' my father's letter.

I went across to the cupboard by the bed and fished it out of the rose-and-stork chamber-pot. It seemed a long time ago, that first night, reading it by candlelight, each word leaping into my mind like sparks from a firework born out of darkness. I sat down in the dusk and read it again, and this time it meant more to me. I could understand his reference to violence, to the shadow, to suicide. I still thought that with an invalid's over-sensitivity he exaggerated the aunts' wish to overpower and crush, but that might well be the half-Braithwaite in me, as he pointed out. In fact, the whole battle was probably a tug of war between his blood and the Braithwaites'.

It was absurd to think like this, really; another excuse.

'If life does not go well for you, think twice before you blame other people . . . never too late to take a new direction. Study your enemies, cherish your friends.'

An odd idea occurred to me. Suppose, if Dunne's theory was correct and there was serial time, then time could be run ahead as well as backwards. Suppose, if I were able to run back the film to that garden of long ago, to see my father lying there writing this letter, then might not he in his long dreaming afternoons have run the film forward? Suppose he had seen me sitting here, alone in my room, led to this inevitable point in time? I read, 'Take another direction.' But there was no reason to do so. Far better to take the same direction, this time with wisdom. Personal relationships were still the greatest challenge. The relationship between a man and a woman contained all the notes in the scale, after all, and if one played them wrong, one had merely to correct the melody, watch the fingering.

All at once I hated myself again. There I went, over-simplifying, taking for granted the fact that Max would agree to my naïve discoveries. The thing to do, the only thing, was to go off alone somewhere, to prove one's independence, grow up by oneself, and only then —

There was a knock on the door, and Aunt Rosa came in. She carried a tray with milk and sandwiches, and as she switched on the light she said, 'Sitting in the dark, dear? And you look so cold.'

I stared at her stupidly. It was entirely unlike Aunt Rosa to carry trays about. She put it down on the bedside cupboard and said, 'Cissie seemed to think you had gone off to bed early. She thought something had upset you.'

'Yes,' I said. 'I mean, no nothing. I'm a bit tired, that's all. Don't worry about me, Aunt Rosa.'

She came and took my hand, chafing it between hers, which were so much smaller and carried several beautiful cool rings.

'Your Aunt Cissie has a sharp tongue, dear, but she doesn't mean all she says. I think her hip has been troubling her today, although she won't admit it. Now you get into bed and I'll send up a hot-water bottle. Oh, and Louie' – she got up to go, and by the door gave me a long grave look that made me feel about ten years old: 'Tomorrow I think you and I should have a talk. Good night, dear, sleep well.'

Like a child, I put a fist into each eye to stop my tears, and realized that for all my good intentions I would be lucky to escape an attack.

I awoke in the middle of the night, sweating. The darkness was suffocating, and outside the window the trees moved restlessly in another kind of darkness. I had dreamed that my grandfather was out there, walking with his guilt, Sir Roger on his shoulder, crooning in his ear, '*Vénus toute entière a sa proie attachée.*' Night after night, across the terrace, over the lawn, along the rose-walks and between the rhododendrons. But never, never along the box hedge to the gate in the wall. Never again, until that early autumn morning when he could bear it no longer and went out with his gun.

I jumped out of bed and switched on the light. Two o'clock. Somewhere an owl called. I would have to read myself to sleep. I climbed back into bed and threw out the cold bottle, which slapped sulkily on to the equally cold linoleum. There was nothing to read except the Buffon I had brought up with me some days ago, to annoy Aunt Rosa. I looked at the beautiful little pictures without seeing them.

There was no proof. Just because a body was discovered at the bottom of the garden, and just because the owner of that garden happened to commit suicide some months later, that didn't mean ... didn't mean ... *couldn't* mean ...

Anyway, it might have been anyone. Bill Protheroe, for

145

instance. He could have left the party at dawn with the others, only by the garden gate instead of by the front door. He could have seen the girl on her way back perhaps, from a stolen night on the common with some boy, and being full of champagne, had tried to kiss her. She would have been startled, got frightened, tried to scream, tried to run. He would have put his hand over her mouth, twisted her neck and there you were. Suddenly she was limp, dead. He would have dropped her by the ditch and run. Then, later, unable to resist it, he would have come by on his usual walk, to find that it was no longer his secret, only his secret guilt.

Did I really believe that? Were girls so easily killed? I didn't know what marks were on her. Her clothes, he had been about to say, were disarranged; that was the classic description of rape. But what were the facts? Was she raped? Was she strangled or bludgeoned or what? A polite tea-party was no place for facts like these; I knew no one would tell me, for now they would not even tell themselves.

I lit a cigarette, lay back and started ticking off the facts. I was now quite wide awake, unfrightened, determined.

My grandfather had been a finicky man, Gibby said. Clean in his habits: overclean. A change of linen twice a day. Well, that fact alone added up to a neat entry in a psychiatrist's notebook. (But would a finicky man commit rape, and go as far as murder?) He was a good shot. I remembered a photograph of him among his friends; a man of middle height, dark, a neat moustache, large and prominent brown eyes, smiling out of his high collar. Small, weak chin. A smoker; with a fastidious taste in pipes. Aunt Seraphina now used one of his pipe racks for storing seeds in test tubes, I remembered. What would he have said to that? There was one pipe I had often admired in a drawer in his desk; the mouthpiece was made of amber, the bowl of ivory was carved into a stag's head, with amber horns set in silver. A dandy's choice. Vanity? How would such a pipe smoke?

Now what else? What about Gwennie? Did he really hanker after young girls, or had she made up the story of the cuddly furs to annoy Aunt Rosa? If it were true, then he could have met the girl at the gate by arrangement, made the usual advances, offered her money, been repulsed, lost his head, slapped her. . . . No one would have seen him run back to the house and up through the garden. But could one be sure? Suppose one of his daughters had come looking for him? Or his wife?

A horrible coldness crawled down my spine. Which one of them had lived with such a thing for so many years? My grandmother? Was that why she had merely turned her head away when I had falsely told her I was to have Max's child? Having seen the worst, once, how could she query lesser misbehaviour, stemming once again from sexual indulgence? She might have told herself with a shrug, 'Les gens, ils sont capable de tout, tout . . .'

Who else? Seraphina, Alec, Bertie, Rosa, my mother, Cissie? The only one I could rule out was Sue, the unborn, the just-conceived. This I would never know. Sir Roger? I remembered the fear, the hatred, on my aunts' faces when I imitated him. He must have seen something; on the night of the great party someone might have forgotten to fasten his chain on his perch, or left the door of his cage open. He would have wandered into the garden, flapping and strutting, and watching. What would he have said, in his hoarse, cynical gabble?

Then there was his namesake, the real Sir Roger. Why had my grandfather so revered the man? Had he admired his work in the Congo and South America? Labour conditions among the natives in remote places would hardly seem to be one of his passionate interests. Casement's reputation then. His positivity, his good looks; he was a man who got things done. How he must have stimulated my grandfather with his free comings and goings and his exuberant

147

conversation! Briefly I wondered whether the two men had had a deeper relationship – but dismissed the idea. It was possible that my grandfather had sensed the other's sexual perversity, and been intrigued by it. Such a subject, however, was in those days kept for secret journals: it was not one gentlemen discussed on a terrace within call of a respectable family.

I had been weaving fantasy for the best part of an hour and was thoroughly chilled. Wearily I put myself through the last few points. Interests: Shooting. The Stock Exchange. The music hall. Reading: Voltaire, Scott, Thackeray, the usual leather-bound gentleman's editions tucked behind glass. A more positive attraction to natural history; to Bewick and Buffon and Gilbert White. His own strange paintings. A passion for general knowledge. 'Your grandfather always ascertained facts,' Aunt Seraphina said once. 'He never let us get away with a slipshod remark. He checked up on everything. Mama said he was encyclopaedia mad.'

Mama said. Do you remember? Mama said. Sue wore her pink hair ribbon, and . . . But why had grandfather never featured in the Game?

Here was my first real clue. Not once had he been re-called. Not once had either of the aunts said, 'Do you remember when dada . . .' When dada what? Beat mama at croquet? Wore his cravat back to front? Nothing. He had no place in the Game. They wanted to forget him and that made him a lonely man.

Do you remember when dada went down the garden to the gate on to the common, raped a servant girl, strangled her, then came back to the house quiet as you please and went to bed with mama in the usual way? Do you remember how one autumn morning he took his gun, and . . .

No, he had no place in the Game, which was a woman's

nostalgic diversion, a web woven of ribbons and emotions, of sentimental, edited memories.

I began to wonder, half asleep, how much he had known, or had guessed, of what went on around him in that house for which he was responsible. All those female activities; the silence of the growing suburb, the stretching gardens, the flower-beds flashing like scimitars among tamed lawns, and among that greater silence the chirping noises of the common lapping up against his garden wall. I saw them all, on still summer afternoons, with all the rooms in the house occupied, my grandfather silently absorbed in his greenhouse; Aunt Seraphina upstairs in her sewing-room, her head buzzing with unrealizable dreams; my mother perhaps playing the piano or going from room to room, singing, her voice snatched out of the windows by a light summer wind. My grandmother, smocking pinafores for the younger children, or working on one of her tapestry panels that now hung in the hall. The boys darting about their own part of the garden, secret among the trees, Sir Roger walking and swaying along a nearby branch. No one, in those long week-ends, would have dreamed of going out; the time for the lemming rush to the sea had not yet arrived. Instead, the house and garden would have vibrated with the energy of its occupants. *The King was in his counting-house, counting out his money; the Queen was in the parlour, eating bread and honey, the maid* . . .

The maids in the kitchen, preparing tea. The tinkle of a bell, and the fragments of the afternoon would come together; from inside and outside, from upstairs and downstairs, the family would assemble on the terrace. Silver teapot, cake-stands, thin bread and butter, conversation as desultory as the humming of bees.

It was an ideal picture, fit for an album, common in an England of that time; and who would want to look below the surface for darkness and violence?

SEVENTEEN

It was to be a busy day. The men were coming to instal Aunt Cissie's television set, and Gibby was expecting Nigel to tea. They were all occupied, so I escaped to the place I had not yet visited: my grandfather's conservatory.

As a child I had called it 'the glass room'. It was there I went to sulk, to draw faces on the dusty panes, or to act out plays on the scrolled-iron platform high above the cobbled yard. It was a splendid place for being Rapunzel and letting down your golden hair. But now I was there for practical reasons. In the intervals of uneasy sleep the night before I had come to some kind of decision; I would make amends, pry no more into the secrets of The Hollies; act responsibly. After all, I told myself, if I was unwilling to come and live here with Max, as Gibby had so strongly hinted I should, then I had no right to disrupt their household, upset their carefully constructed framework. I was there, up in the conservatory, to be constructive: I would clear the place up, so that Aunt Seraphina could use it instead of going off through the wet garden to tend her plants in winter.

Full of energy, and with a clear and peaceful sense of purpose, I tried the door that led into the house, but the bolt had rusted and the wood was warped. It was a carpenter's job. I noticed a rusty bell hanging there: another of my grandmother's ideas, to be rung in case grandfather had 'one of his dizzy turns', for he suffered from high blood pressure, like Aunt Rosa. I was sure he had never rung it, just as sure that it was he who had put the bolt there, on his side. So, like me, he had wanted to escape, and be alone; how he must have resented that door! The aunts had never liked me to go there, either, years ago, because of the dangerous iron spiral stairs. Like too much reading, the wish to be alone was suspect.

It was a misty morning, grey and closed in; the sky an inverted bowl. I was consumed with curiosity about this man who had lived so long ago, and whose life had been blown on so recently by gusts of varying winds, eddying up dead embers. In comparison, the previous obsession with my father had gone; he had put me on the trail and it was due to him that I was here. For although he had never known my grandfather, they shared something; he lying prone under the lilac bushes, reading or writing, the other one up here in this glass box: both escaping from the women of the house.

But I had made the promise not to probe. I went clattering down the iron stairs to fetch a dustpan and brush, a pail of hot water, soap and scrubbing brush and cloths from the scullery. On my return, I saw there was a tap in the corner I had forgotten, with an earthenware sink beneath it, choked with leaves. Above it a pane of glass had broken and damp had rotted the wooden frames. But still, rusty water oozed out of the tap when I turned it on. I felt very much alone; it was like being on the bridge of a becalmed ship. As I brushed off the dirt and cobwebs from the high panes of glass I looked through them at the house next door that stood, like The Hollies, in its half-acre of land, screened by large trees. Some were elms, unsafe in storms. I worked on, wondering what it had been like sixty years ago, when the trees could not have hidden anyone up here. It was a perfect look-out.

The decayed Venetian blinds came down without effort, and the cords snapped in little clouds of rotten fragments. It was a clever idea, that, to control the amount of heat and light that reached his rare plants. Had he done his paintings up here, too? 'Time present and time past,' I told myself comfortingly, 'are both perhaps present in time future.'

And again, 'I am here, or there, or elsewhere. In my beginning.'

Several panes of glass were cracked, so I had to work carefully. I went outside on to the narrow platform to see what I could do with the glass within reach. Without a ladder it was impossible to get to all of it. I looked at the windows above me: that would be Aunt Rosa's bedroom. Above them, the attics; above them, out of sight, the square look-out tower. No one had been up there for years; it was said to be unsafe. How the Victorians loved to build things on to their houses! It was a measure of their confidence. As Max had said, they were born to security and so could plant avenues of trees, throw out gables and turrets, for they did not doubt that their society was founded upon rock and that civilization would endure. This was the secret of their power, and I felt a great nostalgia for it, even though it created other problems which we had inherited; even though it had bred impossible personal relationships.

Exhausted, I went inside and rested against the shelves. They needed scrubbing, too, and I was glad. I needed to use up the physical energy that was flowing strongly through me. I swept the dust and leaves on to the floor and started to sweep them up, crushing small black spiders that ran out with their cold secretiveness. Wanting to make a thorough job of it, I crawled underneath the shelves with a hand-brush, but caught my hair on a nail. Reaching up to pull free, a loose board came out and upset some pots of soil that had been pushed far back and forgotten. Picking up the board I felt clips on the underside and turned it over. Attached to it was a long, solid tube in a leather case, black with dust and damp, a leather cap at either end. I was full of guilty excitement and an odd despair. *I wasn't looking*, I said aloud, to no one. Then I undid the straps with difficulty and pulled out a telescope.

For a moment I was puzzled, then I did what anyone

would have done: pulled it out full-length and put it to my eye. Everything was a blur. So, although the eyepiece was still bright and clean, I wiped it, adjusted the focus and tried again.

At once the common swam right up to me. It was astonishing. I could see every bush and tree; children a long way off threw a ball in my direction so that I ducked, expecting to hear their cries. I took the telescope outside and stood there, looking in every direction, delighted with this new toy. It was like being a deaf god, seeing without hearing; seeing without being seen. I looked through the windows of the next-door attic and saw stored shelves of apples inside. In a room below a woman rested on her bed with cottonwool pads over her eyes. At once I turned away, only to look back a moment later with a pouncing pleasure.

It was then, as if a hand had been placed on my shoulder and lips placed to my ear, that I understood my grandfather. Here we both stood, sharing vicariously in the forbidden life of the common, of other people's bedrooms. Here we stood, on a grey autumn day, all eyes; watching, watching. We were not so different from the children below who had once watched, secret among leaves, although their spying had been innocent. I was on the edge of this dead man's cold world, seeing but not sharing, and the terrible emptiness of it blew through me like an icy draught.

I could not move, could not lower this third eye. Mechanically I noted that a man dug potatoes at the bottom of the next garden, shook them free of soil, tossed them into a bowl. Then, across our own lawn, came Aunt Rosa, calling. I could see that she had on her thin house slippers and that if she went any further over the grass, they would be soaking wet. I called to her, thinking she was nearer than she actually was, waved. Uncertainly she looked about her, then her face was towards me, she seemed to look straight into my eyes. I saw her face turn grey, saw her stagger, and fall.

I threw the thing aside and stampeded down the stairs. As I ran across the garden to her—it seemed a long, long way—I realized with horror that this was the second time I had unwittingly frightened her. And this time, I knew, she would never believe I had not intended it.

She must have given a faint cry, for Gibby had heard, and now came running across the lawn, a small bottle in her hand.

'Her pills – give her her pills. It must be a heart attack. Lift her head and put these in her mouth. Quick, child.'

We supported her head, and slowly she seemed to recover. Her slipper had been wrenched off, and the grass was scarred. Gibby and I crouched beside her on the wet ground until her eyes opened. But she did not look at me. She put out a hand to Gibby and only with reluctance allowed me to ease on her slipper, put my arm around her waist and help her slowly, step by step, back to the house.

When we had laid her on Gibby's old sofa, I put the kettle on.

'She was coming to call you,' said Gibby. 'The men are here, they want to fix an aerial or something. Miss Seraphina is in a state.'

Aunt Rosa did not speak until Gibby had made the tea and handed her a cup.

'Take some in to them in Cissie's room,' she said. 'Louise will help me to the morning-room. I must rest there.'

'Don't move, Aunt Rosa. Not yet.'

When Gibby had gone with her tray she turned to me, the cup shaking in her hand. 'Where is it? What have you done with it? I could never find it. . . .'

'Let me hold that cup for you,' I said. 'I don't know what you mean. Find what? What happened out there? Do you often have these attacks? I must call the doctor.'

But her hand grasped my wrist as I held the cup, and we were latched together, her eyes behind her spectacles enlarged and almost beyond sight.

'I want you. I want to talk to you. By ourselves.'

'Yes, when you're better. Don't move yet.'

'Don't tell Seraphina. No doctor. I came to call you. Oh, my God! Go in to them. Say nothing.'

To my horror she took off her spectacles and began to cry, mopping away at her defenceless eyes with a small handkerchief.

Gibby said, coming in, 'She's upset. She'll be all right. I'll see to her. You'd better go in, Miss Lou, or there'll be a free fight.'

I went, reluctantly. As I opened the door of the study Aunt Seraphina was saying, 'You're not tearing my father's study to pieces just to put that rubbish in.'

Two red-faced, embarrassed men were standing behind a large television set, cornered and defensive. They held Gibby's kitchen cups in their hands, and tried to drink the tea as if they wanted it. Watching them, and each other with hostility, were my two aunts. When they saw me everyone began speaking at once.

'This is *my* room now, and —'

'It's like this, miss. We've got to connect this set to something, haven't we, and the lead's got to go —'

'Toenails!' cried Aunt Seraphina, pouncing on to the carpet, 'Toenails in dada's study! Disgusting! You never know where it'll end.'

Aunt Cissie manœuvred her chair across the room and as she went a small bell tinkled. Gibby must have found one for her and fastened it on.

'Don't be absurd, Seraphina,' she said, white with rage, and clenching her fists as if she would like to strike that bent head. 'Get up from the floor this instant, the men will think you are mad. Now, Louise, kindly explain to your aunt that

155

if the set is not put in today I shall go straight back to Eastbourne.'

'And good riddance!' flashed Aunt Seraphina, still on all-fours, 'Turning the house upside-down, coming here with your airs and graces. There's another! Oh, it's disgusting!'

The men watched in petrified silence. The atmosphere was so tense that I could have laughed had I not remembered Aunt Rosa in the kitchen, abdicating from authority with her grey face and her tears.

'Just a moment, Aunt Seraphina,' I said, 'Would you go to Aunt Rosa? She's in the kitchen with Gibby. She's had a slight heart attack and needs care. Please be calm with her.'

At once Seraphina stood up. Nervously she began to rub her thumb against her fingers, discarding whatever it was she had picked up from the carpet. They might indeed have been little crescent toenails, for I had cut Aunt Cissie's nails for her a night or two ago.

'Oh, no,' she said. 'Oh, no.' She looked at us, lost, as if we were strangers. 'It's all this fuss. I'll go to her. Oh, my poor girl.' And she went from the room slowly, as if a spring had broken.

At once the older of the two men began to explain. The bell on Aunt Cissie's chair tinkled as she went from place to place as the men indicated what would have to be done, and she turned the revolving table with the set on it, and viewed the dead screen from all angles.

'It isn't as if there'll be much mess,' the younger man said, pushing his long gingery hair back from a pink scalp. 'There's no need for the other lady to be upset. The wires will go flat against this panelling, see. We'll just have to bore a hole through this wall and find a place for the outside aerial and there you are. You've got a power point here, so there'll be nothing to trip you.'

'Do it quickly then,' I told them, 'before my aunt comes back. She's elderly, you see, and . . .'

'That's all right, miss,' he said. 'My grannie's a bit funny. You've got to go easy with old people.' He looked apologetically at Aunt Cissie, but she did not appear to have heard. As they started to work, she beckoned me over.

'How bad is Rosa?' she asked. 'Have you called a doctor?'

'She said there was no need. She seems better now, but she must rest.'

My aunt looked at me oddly, and I knew what she was thinking: the decision should have been mine. She was right, so I at once went out into the hall and looked up the doctor's number in the small blue notebook, marked on the cover, in capitals, IMPORTANT NUMBERS. He said he would call round at lunch-time, and to keep her quiet. As I turned away from the telephone I was aware that, in spite of the upset day, the feeling of physical well-being was still running strongly through me. I felt, perhaps for the first time in my life, that it was I, not anyone else, running this house. The aunts were my responsibility, I had ceased to be theirs. As if to underline this curious conviction, I heard the door of the morning-room open and then close, and Aunt Seraphina was speaking to me, in a quiet voice.

'I've wrapped her up warm. She's lying on mama's old love-seat. She wants to see you when you can spare the time.'

I nodded, then stopped her as she went past. It was essential to prevent her from going into Aunt Cissie's room while the men were working.

'Aunt Seraphina,' I said, taking her arm, 'Do you know of a carpenter?'

'A carpenter, why?'

'To get that door open on the second landing. The one that goes through into grandfather's conservatory. I'm cleaning it out for you, to save you a journey over the garden in the winter. I thought we might move your plants up there.'

She stared at me in astonishment, and I saw that she had forgotten the men in Aunt Cissie's room.

'Move my flowers? Use dada's conservatory? Why, it's been shut for years . . . years, Louie. I don't think . . .'

But she smiled. She was pleased. I saw pleasure and excitement flicker over her tensed mouth, and her taut hands relaxed. 'Why, Louie, how kind! You've cleared it out, you say? I used to spend hours up there as a child. We kept it spotless. But mama shut it up; she put a curtain over the door. Because of the draught, she said. I could never have used it while she was alive.' Uncertainty was making her nervous again, but the idea had hold of her, and resolution quickened her into speech. 'But, of course, it would be . . . Yes, better for my exotics altogether. I could have a small oil-stove. Oh . . .' her mouth went down, 'but the green blinds must have dropped to pieces. I could never regulate the sun. Dada was so particular about the sun.'

'Then my Christmas present to you will be new blinds. We'll have them fitted.'

A faint voice called from behind the closed door, and with a nervous glance Aunt Seraphina said, 'Rosa would never allow it.'

I grasped my aunt's arm, knowing, with pity, how many things had been denied her because either my grandmother or Aunt Rosa would never allow it. The ghost of Bruno, the man she had once loved and had given up, the man who had given me brandy at the play in the park, and had then vanished; her lost career as a singer: these things made me say, positively, commandingly:

'See to it now. Have the door opened as soon as you can. After all, you're the one who keeps the house full of flowers. It's your pleasure. Do it and see what happens then.' Cunningly, perhaps unwisely, I added, 'After all, Aunt Cissie has her television.'

At once she flushed, then left me as Gibby called her from the kitchen with some question about lunch. I turned the handle of the morning-room door and went in for my talk with Aunt Rosa. If I had known what was coming, I would have thanked God for my new-found strength.

EIGHTEEN

SHE LOOKED so much better, propped up against the cushions in the chintz-covered love-seat by the window, that my momentary qualm of conscience about the small rebellion I had started in the hall died at once. Aunt Seraphina had wrapped her warmly in a large fleecy shawl, and there was a hot-water bottle at her feet. A small fire was burning and before I went over to her I put on more coal.

She sat, with a composed grave face, and her first words surprised me.

'So you think we haven't been fair to you?'

I knew then that she and Aunt Cissie had been talking.

'You want to know everything about us. That is why you came home?' Not home, I told myself. Back. 'You've been ferreting about, Louise. It wasn't nice of you.. If there were things you wanted to know, why didn't you ask me?'

'Because you wouldn't have told me. You've never told me anything.'

She closed her eyes, picked at her shawl with her fingers, and looked old. She seemed to consider the statement, then nodded.

'You were too young. You ran off and left us. Why should I tell you? You left the family. We've scarcely seen you alone since. It grieved your grandmother terribly; she never got over it.'

I had to sit down near her, and now I moved uneasily on my low chair, at a disadvantage, stung by this accusation, which was just.

'Aunt Rosa, I know it was all too sudden. I was young. But as it happened, it's worked out all right. At least, I think so—'

She gave a small, almost soundless laugh.

'*You* think so! You know even less about men than you do about this family. How do you know what Max is doing while you spend your time here, trying to find out about things that happened in the past, long before you were born? My child, you don't know anything, and that's why – you're sure the door is closed? – I'm going to tell you what I think you have a right to know.'

She had made me angry, so I said loudly, 'Yes, I have a right! You must trust me. I'm a Braithwaite too, remember, like you and Aunt Seraphina —'

'Seraphina knows nothing. She has never known the whole truth – nor must she ever know. She lives in a world of her own. She is not strong enough to bear some things. Only mama and I know. And I am only telling you now to help you to understand your husband, and my poor father. . . .' She had been looking out of the window, a low bay which faced the gravel drive at the front of the house, but now she turned to me and said with compelling dignity, 'I don't want to tell you, either, but you force my hand, and nothing is ever done with. And because you always had an imagination, like your father – all that reading – you might think wild things, dreadful things that are not true.'

She was looking at me as she spoke, and I felt my hands go clammy and cold. All at once I was afraid of what I might hear. I had a feeling that after she had told me I would never be the same again. But then, neither would she, and that gave me courage.

'But I want your solemn promise, Louise, not to let this go outside the family. Let it die with you. Not even your father knew, nor your mother. You are not to tell Max.'

At the involuntary expression that crossed my face, she said, 'Very well. Then it remains my secret. Think what you like, I have nothing to say.'

So the shadow was not to lengthen. I said at last, painfully, 'All right. I won't tell Max.'

'You promise? There's no need, you see. It wouldn't be important to him. Only to us. Only to the Braithwaites.'

'Aunt Rosa, I do know a little. The Protheroes —'

'Your Aunt Cissie told me. But they do not know the end. I was so upset, so angry. . . . But who told you about your grandfather? The other thing – the last thing?'

'It was in a letter my father left for me at the solicitor's.'

'So *that* was it! I blamed Gibby.'

'Gibby had nothing to do with it.' This small lie at least I owed to Gibby.

She lay back, closed her eyes and said, 'Now don't interrupt me, because I can only tell this once. Then perhaps I can – forget it.'

'I must have been a girl of eighteen,' said Aunt Rosa. 'That was before the Great War, of course. Your grandfather spent hours up in that greenhouse place of his, either alone, or with Seraphina, experimenting with rare plants. His ambition was to succeed in getting a particular Chinese lily to bloom in this country. I believe his friend, Sir Roger Casement, brought him the bulbs – don't ask me how he got them, because I don't know. He wanted to write a paper about it for some botanical society. Mama used to wonder what he found to do all those hours up in that place of his. She scarcely ever saw him. She didn't mind him being in the study, which was right for a man. How she cried, poor soul, when he put the bolt on the inside of the door. They had such words.

' "It's like Bluebeard's locked room, Rosie," she would say to me sometimes. I was the only one she could speak to, being the eldest. "Find out what he does. It isn't nice, I'm sure, for a man to shut himself away from his family. Suppose he had a heart attack all alone up there?"

'So I used to go out into the garden and watch, just for fun, really. It was then I used to see him up there with that telescope. That was why you gave me such a turn this morning. Some days he'd stand for hours, looking this way and that. Out over the common, into people's gardens . . .'

(Into servants' attic bedrooms, I added silently.)

'Sometimes he'd go up to the tower and watch from there. Of course there was no harm to it, as I thought then. But you must understand, Louie, that some men are strange in their minds. They like to watch other people – well, when those people don't know they are being watched. It isn't nice, it isn't nice at all, dear, and I'm sorry for them. It's the way they're made. You won't mind my saying this, as you're married, but even a man's body is untidy. And one day such a rough man came to the door, shouting. Someone had been watching him and his girl in the bushes, he said. If he wanted to go into the bushes with his girl, it wasn't anybody's business, but he'd caught the glint of a telescope from the glass thing on the side of our house. Of course your grandfather refused to see the fellow, and when the maid called mama, she threatened to call the police. Well, that sort of thing was very unpleasant, of course. I don't expect your grandfather meant any harm: it was just his way. But mama changed towards him after that, she —'

She stopped talking, as if she feared what she might say. From somewhere outside I thought I heard men tramping upstairs, but dismissed the idea. I had no cigarettes with me, and did not like to break the thread by suggesting that I fetched them. I felt curiously detached, and longed to smoke. After a moment Aunt Rosa went on again.

'Well, that dreadful night. The party night. A lot of people came, and we had a buffet supper on the terrace, a little music, and Seraphina sang. Then we went up through the house to the conservatory to see the lily bloom. I remember mama saying that now he could be grateful to her for having the door put through; we couldn't have gone up those spiral stairs in the dark. And your grandfather was beside himself with excitement. He insisted on toasting the lily in champagne. The blooms kept coming one after the other, unfolding all through the night. "Look," he kept saying, "It never stops. Again and again, one after the other. The bud, the flower, the fading, marvellous, marvellous!" And all our guests, who didn't know a thing about botany, went on drinking and shouting as the flowers opened. All through the night it went on, and the last one faded before dawn, they told me afterwards.

'I was sent off to bed about one o'clock; the younger children had gone about an hour before, and Seraphina made a great fuss; she wanted to stay to the end. But of course she couldn't be allowed; she was too young, thank God. I woke up as the last of the guests were going, and looked out of my window – you know it's just above dada's greenhouse. I stayed there a long time, my head was throbbing with the champagne and the excitement, and I saw the dawn come up. The common looked pink, I remember, and it was then I saw dada just below me on the iron platform with his telescope. I stayed watching him as he looked through it, and I thought how tired he must be. Suddenly he dropped it and gave a terrible cry. Not loud: it was more of a groan, as if he were in pain. I thought he was having a fit and would fall from the platform, so I put on a dressing-gown and went down to the door on the landing.'

Aunt Rosa stopped. She was very pale, and I was afraid. I put a hand over one of hers and found it cold. After a moment she moved it away and nodded, as if she was all right. I watched her lips moving; it seemed to me that we were in the middle of an enchanted, unreal circle.

'I turned the handle and went in. He was on his knees, his

head on the shelf among the flowerpots, sobbing. Have you ever seen a man cry, Louie? It's the most terrible thing in the world. Like the sky falling, or God saying that He's the Devil. I was only eighteen, remember, and I went down on my knees, too, put my arms round him and cried with him. He kept saying things I couldn't understand – I've forgotten them now – and then he was sick. When I offered to fetch mama, he nearly went mad. "Don't tell her or she'll think I did it," he kept on saying, "They'll all think I did it." '

(Of course, I whispered to myself, of course. He couldn't have done it. People who watch don't do.)

'Then he told me what he'd seen. Just by the gate there. A big man. This girl. He wanted to go down and see what he could do, call the police. I said no, stay here, go to bed. It was the scandal, you see, Louise, the scandal. It was bad enough having such a thing happen almost in our garden, but fancy people saying that Mr Braithwaite had found the —. Had found it.'

'How did you know she was dead?' I had to ask this, out of pure horror.

My aunt moved her stiff mouth.

'I went to see,' she said. 'I gave dada some brandy, and in some queer way made him think it was a dream. He went to bed, but stayed in his dressing-room on the day-bed there, not to disturb mama. I had some brandy myself, and then I went down into the garden, and the birds were singing. It was going to be a beautiful day.' She gave a little smile. 'You see, Louie, I didn't really believe him. I thought he'd drunk too much – and it was such a glorious morning. Even when I saw her I only half-believed it. So then I was sick, too.'

'Was she strangled?' I had to know. I would not allow myself to feel pity for that eighteen-year-old until I knew.

Aunt Rosa nodded.

'She looked so young. One black stocking torn half off, her skirt torn . . . But Louie, all I thought about was dada.

What would happen in the morning. The full shock came later; I was in bed for days seeing that girl's face.'

She pulled off her rings one by one, then put them back on again. I thought: thank God it was Aunt Rosa, not Aunt Seraphina. She'd have gone mad. As it was I could not take my eyes off her. Soft, pink Aunt Rosa.

'I was wrong, Louie. It wasn't honest. I shouldn't have persuaded dada against his duty. It preyed on his mind, and first he destroyed the lily, because in some way he blamed it. Then, months later, he did this terrible thing. He was ill, you see, he felt guilty. . . .'

No, she was wrong. It was the peak of his life; his only regret must have been that he had never been able to do this thing himself. The logical end to the sexual act. The last bloom.

She was saying, 'It took them more than a year to find the murderer. A man from the asylum over the hill. He escaped and tried it again and was caught. Then he told them what he'd done before he was put away. It made me understand about men, Louie. I feel so sorry for them; a woman's world is so much more comfortable. We're comfortable in this house – now. Although of course we can never forget —'

'Yes, you can, Aunt Rosa. You can forget, because you understand. And I want you to do something for me. Let Aunt Seraphina use the conservatory. Let that door be opened again. The only way to let the past lie is to let it grow into the present.' I couldn't help quoting again, '"Time present and time past are both perhaps present in time future."'

'I can't make anything of that,' said Aunt Rosa. 'All that sort of talk is above my head, I don't pretend to understand it. But now you know everything. Now you know what responsibility a woman bears when a man confides in her utterly. I didn't want it, and I suppose it spoilt my life, but it made me understand. You see, Louie, a woman has power; she can make or break a man. Mama never understood that.

I think she was frightened of dada, but it wasn't for me to judge. Mind you understand your Max, now, because he's a good man.' She stared out of the window at the invincible holly bushes. 'Poor dada,' she spoke almost to herself. 'Crying there – he cracked apart in my hands. I would have left home if he hadn't put an end to himself.'

As she was speaking, one of those curious half-remembered pieces of information that one supposes to be forgotten floated to the surface of my mind. I had once wanted to go to Mexico, and had accordingly read a great deal about the Aztecs. Now I remembered the name of a goddess, Tlasoltetl, the Eater of Filth. But she was also known as the Mother of the Gods. Alone of all the earth goddesses, she had a moral significance; by eating refuse, which symbolized the sins of mankind, she purified the human race. It was strange, bizarre even, to think of Aunt Rosa in this context, but it had arisen spontaneously; and why not? Perhaps, by understanding the poor frightened child imprisoned behind my grandfather's Victorian façade, she had absorbed his sins and purified him. I remembered then that confession had become part of the goddess's cult. Stranger things happened, but no name was given to them. We had not progressed so very far in thousands of years.

We sat together with no more words to be said, and at last there was a tap on the door and Gibby came in, looking bothered.

'The doctor's here, Miss Rosa,' she said. 'I didn't send for him, I'm sure. Shall I ask him to come in?'

'I sent for him,' I said, getting up. 'I thought it wise.'

'Ask him to come in, Gibby,' said Aunt Rosa: 'not that it was necessary.'

But she did not seem annoyed, and as the doctor went in I followed Gibby into the hall.

'Lunch is almost ready, Miss Lou. Fancy you sending for Dr Davidson without permission! Well, I don't know . . . And all that coming and going upstairs: Miss Seraphina's in a rare state. Pleased, mind you. And they've put the aerial up on the roof somewhere. I do hope folks won't see it. Looks so common, stuck up on chimneys, I always think.'

'What on earth are they doing now, though?'

Gibby was thoroughly put out. She had begun to tell me, when Aunt Cissie's bell rang along the passage. She came up to us and said at once, 'We shall all be able to look in tonight. Gibby, you'll come too, won't you? We shall be so cosy. And Louie, would you pop out, dear, for the *Radio Times* this afternoon? We must be informed.'

Before Gibby or I could reply, there was a splintering sound from upstairs, some banging, and Aunt Seraphina's high, excited laugh.

'I don't know what this house is coming to,' muttered Gibby. 'I don't know, and that's a fact. We were always so quiet.' But her eyes were bright as she turned to me and said, as Aunt Cissie went whisking away again to her room, 'Fancy, did you hear *that*, Miss Lou! That's one for the book. Askin' me in of an evening. That'll be something to tell my boy Nige. Not that I hold with too much of it, mind, but now and again it'll make a change, like the pictures. Come on now, dearie, what are we talking here for? Meal'll be spoiled, else.'

'I'll come and set the table for you, Gibby,' I said, and was about to follow her when the doctor came out of the morning-room.

'She'll be all right,' he said. 'But it's always chancy, a heart like hers. I could give her five years or five months; she'll just have to take it easy. Let her rest for today, though, she's got her pills for an emergency. Where's this other aunt of yours I've been asked to see while I'm here? Broken hip, wheelchair? I don't remember her.'

'Oh, you mean Aunt Cissie. I'll take you to her; but if you're not expected you'll get a pretty hot reception.'

I led him to the door of Aunt Cissie's room and left him, cravenly. Then I ran upstairs to the second landing, suddenly remembering the telescope.

The conservatory was buzzing with activity. The door stood open and light poured on to the landing and the stairs. The older of the two men was trying to smooth off the splintered door frame, and the young ginger-haired assistant was climbing up the iron spiral stairs with an armful of plants. Aunt Seraphina had lost no time. She stood by the shelves, finishing off the sweeping-up.

'I couldn't finish it,' I said. 'I'm so sorry. I'll scrub them for you after lunch. By the way, Aunt Seraphina, it's nearly on the table.'

'Oh, I'm too excited to eat, dear,' she said. 'Isn't it kind of Mr Jones? He insisted on helping me with the plants. There's water here, too, Louie. . . . Do you know, I'd forgotten. What a good idea of yours!' She pushed back a grey hair and left a streak of dust on her cheek. The cross and nagging woman of a few hours ago, pouncing on toenails, might never have existed.

The young man put his load down carefully on the nearest shelf, grinning at me. 'I've only got one more lot to bring, m'm,' he said to my aunt. 'I'll just fetch them up now; then we'll all knock off for our dinners.'

I hurried after him, picking up the leather case from the floor. Luckily, Aunt Seraphina had not noticed it. The telescope had rolled to the edge of the platform, caught against a whorl of iron in the railings, and I picked it up and went down the spiral stairs. I had to get rid of it somehow. I came up with the ginger-haired young man by the shrubbery and waited until we were out of sight of the house. As he turned round, surprised, I said, 'Look, I'm sorry the aunts were difficult. . . . You've been so kind; it means a great deal to

Aunt Seraphina to have her plants carried up for her. Will you take – I mean, I'd like you to have this.' As he hesitated, ready to be affronted, I added, 'You can see for miles.'

I had forgotten that ginger-haired people blushed so easily. Now the colour of his embarrassment flooded up to his hairline and he blurted out, 'Oh, no, that's all right. Your aunt's bark is worse than her bite. I'm glad to help.'

'Try it,' I said. 'Look, you adjust the focus like this,' and I forced him to take it. If he refused I would have to bury it somewhere and it might turn up again, years later. I wanted to end it all, now.

Reluctantly he raised the telescope to his eye and aimlessly sighted a tree. When he lowered it he held it with a new respect, almost the respect of ownership, and said, 'Cor! I could see every feather of that bird up there. Marvellous.'

'Well, then, do have it. There's no one here who can use it now. Are you married?'

He was turning the long brass tube over in his hand.

'Lovely job. They knew how to make things in them days, didn't they? Married? Yes, I'm married, miss. Baby comin' and all. Well, if you're sure . . . thanks very much.'

'Your son might like it one day. He could play at sailors with it.'

We stood in silence, thinking of our separate futures. Then he gave me a slow smile and handed it back. For a moment I thought he meant to change his mind, but instead he told me to have a look at the aerial.

'It's right behind that tower up there. Your aunts were most particular it shouldn't be seen from the road.' He shrugged and watched as I put the telescope to my eye for the last time. The tower came strongly into vision; square and challenging and unsafe, like an undeserved crown. By it the abstract pattern of the aerial gesticulated frailly against the grey autumn sky.

NINETEEN

THE HOUSE seemed empty after the men had gone. Aunt Rosa had her lunch in the morning-room, on a tray, then settled down for a sleep. My other two aunts were resting, too, and in the kitchen Gibby and I cleaned and polished in preparation for Nigel. As she started to bake some little cakes and biscuits (a big one would take too long, she grumbled, she'd had no time with all the coming and going), I set off across the common to buy the *Radio Times* for Aunt Cissie, and to add it to the regular newspaper order.

It was late when I walked back again. I had gone the long way round, walking slowly, eating a bar of chocolate, and thinking. The morning seemed a long way off, almost in another time, and the heavy greyness had not lifted, so that each bush and tree appeared solid and drab. I felt I had no part in it; it had done with me. Tomorrow, I told myself, if Aunt Rosa were better, tomorrow I would telephone to Max. I would not need to explain.

I think, as I walked over the dull waste of my childhood places, that I finally digested the Braithwaites, and I wondered at the fury of my previous state. I felt, as I went slowly towards the backs of the long gardens, as a soldier might walking over an old battlefield, asking himself if it had all been worth the noise and the suffering. It was then that, unprepared, I saw the two old people sitting on the seat by the cut. Sunset was near, and a sullen pink glow split the heavy clouds. Recognition and fear hammered respectively in my brain and my belly. I could not stop my leaden feet walking, as in the dream, and as I approached the seat the old man pushed out a long, unclean brown boot.

I was only about ten yards away now, and again, as in the

dream, I scanned the wall of the garden, the house, and there was the glass conservatory, reflecting what was left of the sinking sun. It was exactly as I had always dreamed it. I must go nearer; the old man wanted me to trip over that boot: I always did. Then they would get up, slowly, and then . . .

I forced myself to look up into their faces. The boot withdrew. The man rose, tall, rigid, to his feet.

'Why, Louise, what are you doing, out on the common at this time of night?' asked old Mr Protheroe.

I sank down beside them, weak, unable to speak. Then I flapped the copy of the *Radio Times* in explanation, said good evening to Miss Protheroe, and told them that we had at last had a television set put in for Aunt Cissie.

'Perhaps you'd give us your arm up the cut,' said Miss Protheroe, after telling me all about the joy their television set had brought them. 'We shouldn't have come out, such a heavy day. But Willie insisted. It's too damp for his constitutional. Too damp so early. And the evenings draw in so.'

Only her battered old brown felt hat had any connection with the woman in the dream, and I felt nothing more than a passing tremor as she reached out for my arm.

'Yes, soon be winter,' said her brother. 'We used to skate on the ponds, do you remember, Lucy? Now I remember your father, young lady, before his illness, his figure-of-eights were the best I've seen.'

'Once we waltzed,' said Lucy, picking up her handbag and holding on to me while we waited for Mr Protheroe to join us. 'Seraphina brought out a portable gramophone and we danced. Tum-tum-tum-te-tum . . .' she hummed. 'We had fun in those days.'

'Might as well be dead now,' said old Mr Protheroe. 'We're in the book, but we've lost the page we're on.' His hard old hand dug into my arm. 'Eh, maybe we're all dead and don't know it. Ever thought of that, Louise? Eh? eh?'

Hadn't Aunt Seraphina once used the same expression?

'I don't think any of us know exactly what page we're on, Mr Protheroe,' I said. 'Anyway, it's easy to lose the place.'

They chuckled as if I had made some rare witticism, and we set off. When we reached the cut I went ahead with Miss Protheroe, and the old man had to follow us, using his stick jerkily. She took the opportunity to whisper, 'It's too far for him to walk, but he's always been obstinate. How long are you staying with your aunts, dear?'

'Not much longer,' I replied. 'Why not pop in and see them? Aunt Rosa wasn't well this morning, but she's better now.'

But the idea of dropping in uninvited frightened Miss Protheroe. 'Oh no, oh no,' she said, obviously put out. 'I'll give them a ring in the morning. Rosa hasn't been at all well lately. Getting old, poor soul. We all are.'

I felt a hard poke at waist level and looked round to catch old Mr Protheroe's petrified leer. He had overheard his sister's last remark.

'Ah, but you're not old, are you, my dear? You're still young and fresh. Young and fresh. But all milk sours in time, remember that.'

I took them to the end of the road, to where Chestnut Crescent began, and watched them as they went along slowly, keeping near the hedges. A most unfrightening old couple. An old couple, however, I wanted no longer, in my dreams or out of them. I walked back to the house, passed the front gates and again went down the cut. I leaned against the wall by the tradesmen's entrance and felt weak. It had taken a good deal of will-power to walk up the cut with old Mr Protheroe close behind, breathing dry, resentful lust down my neck, and I had been glad of poor silly Lucy on my arm. All they had wanted of me was my youth, and a witness to their memories.

I opened the gate slowly and went along the gravel path

until I reached the lighted kitchen windows. Looking in, I saw that Gibby and Nigel had finished their tea, and that he was holding up something for his mother to admire. Gibby sat back and watched him, her dark little eyes non-committal. As I pushed open the door I heard his impatient voice.

'Really, mum, you give me a pain. Look at the value. Go on, take a look for yourself. It's not rubbish, is it? Go on, feel it.'

I pushed aside the green serge curtain as Nigel was thrusting a blue teddy-bear into his mother's face, rubbing it up and down against her cheek in an exasperated parody of affection. They both looked round as I came in and Gibby gave her son a meaning look, lifting up her head strongly, as if by this means she could urge him to his feet. Reluctantly he rose from the table, as reluctantly took half a step towards me. We shook hands and I gave him what I hoped was a warm, welcoming smile.

'Well, Nigel, what a long time! I don't think I've seen you since I was a little girl. I used to come to tea, do you remember?'

He nodded grudgingly, and Gibby suddenly gave a little cough of laughter.

'You and the pink newspaper, Miss Lou! Do you remember that? Fred never forgot it, bless him. Often had a laugh over it, the two of us.'

Of course I remembered; the aunts, too, had thought it a great joke. Now Gibby had to tell it all over again for Nigel's benefit, but I knew it wouldn't amuse him.

'We used to have squares of newspaper strung up in the lavatory in the yard, you know, Nige. And the first time Miss Lou came to tea – oh, she was quite a nipper then, couldn't have been more'n six – she asked why they were pink. Never seen a pink newspaper, she hadn't, and why should she? So Fred said that it was because he was a racing man. Took it all in, but I never thought she'd remember it.

But that night she told her Aunt Seraphina that she'd learned something important, and did she know that all racing men had pink newspapers in their lavatories?'

Gibby went off into hiccups of laughter, and Nigel smiled thinly. I felt a fool, for the story would merely re-affirm his early opinion of my precocity. I had never got on with him, and he did not seem to have changed much since our first meeting. He had a hard, coarse face, small clever black eyes, a flat head emphasized by the black hair that lay flatly brushed across it, pressed, almost steamed, into the skull by the weight of grease that lay on it. His voice, too, was hard and very quick and precise, as if he wanted to throw away a series of very clever asides and yet regretted doing so. Not coarse, though, that voice. Somewhere education had crept in and done things to its vowels and tonal values. Now, in early middle age, he neighed like a schoolmaster, whereas years ago he would merely have whined nasally. He had, I noticed, none of the natural good manners his father had possessed, and none of Gibby's simple goodness. He resented us all, and was now suffering by being caught having tea in the kitchen.

To hide my nervousness, for no one is at ease while being actively disliked, I pointed foolishly to the blue bear.

'What on earth's that?' It came out patronizingly, and at once he was on the defensive.

'What's it look like, then?' He spoke off-handedly, as he used to years ago when I asked him simple questions about his Meccano set. 'There's these new trading stamps; we've got the idea from America. Super bear, that is. One book. My wife saves 'em all the time. Marvellous things we've got. Whistling kettle, red. Zipped-up shopper, tricycle for the nipper. Now this bear for the baby. And now we're saving up for —'

'You don't get anything for nothing,' broke in Gibby firmly, pushing the bear contemptuously with her finger.

'You never know what's in 'em. What's this stuffed with, then? You'll give the baby an illness. S'pose its eyes come out and baby swallows 'em, eh?'

'It's nylon fur, mum. Washable nylon. What's wrong with it? The eyes are all right.' In desperation he picked up the bear and shook it. For a moment I thought he was going to gouge open the seams to show us the super-hygienic stuffing.

'Doesn't even growl,' said Gibby with quiet satisfaction.

'How's the family, Nigel?' I asked hastily.

'Can't complain. Doing very nicely. Eldest boy's in the grammar school now. He'll have a better chance than I did.' He saw his mother's face and said quickly, 'No offence, mum. What chance was there in my day? The tin school or nothing. I've no complaints. I've worked my way up.'

'He's assistant manager now,' said Gibby. She was at a loss with her quick son. His moods seemed to change so. I wondered whether he had been bullying her to go and live with him.

'Yes, we've got a nice house on a council estate. One of the new ones. Our name came up last year. We're out at Reading now. Not far with a car, of course.'

'He's got a car and all,' said Gibby.

'Things have changed.' Nigel nodded, boring into me with his little black eyes. He seemed to make a decision, for he turned his back on his mother and spoke passionately, right at me.

'No beating about the bush, Miss – er, Mrs —'

'Yeovil.'

'Mrs Yeovil. I don't want my mother to go on working all her life, now that dad's gone. And what with them pulling down the house and all that I don't see why she shouldn't come and live with us. We've got room. There's a garden. She can watch telly. Kids'll keep her young. Iris wants her to come – I told you that, didn't I, mum? – I want her to come.

But will she? She will not. What's she got to keep her here?' He looked round at the big comfortable kitchen with loathing. 'Blooming great house for three old women, doesn't make sense. You could put four families in this house and lose 'em. Why work at her age?'

'That's enough, Nige. Miss Lou knows why if you don't. And that's enough. I said it's enough —'

'She's got her own family to see to, her own flesh and blood,' Nigel broke in, in a rage. 'She's got grandchildren. Why should she slave for other people?'

I suppressed a smile, for the kernel of his argument lay exposed. For all his cleverness he went on to ruin his chances.

'Iris could do a nice little job if mum'd come. It'd mean more money. But no. Everyone else's kids but her own!'

That was one for me. 'Where's your telly then?' he demanded furiously, turning on his mother as if she were a blackleg at a union meeting. 'You can ask for a telly, you know. What do you do in the evenings without a telly? *They've* got one. Do they let you watch it?'

'It was only put in today,' said Gibby mildly. 'I'm watching it this evening. We all are, and very nice too, if you like that sort of thing all the time. There's my own wireless on the dresser. We're never bored in this house, Nigel, don't you think that, my boy. We haven't forgotten the use of our hands, like some people. I knit winter woollies for the children, don't I? And how can I turn a sock if I'm gawping at a screen?'

Nigel had been getting restless while she was speaking; obviously he did not like other people to make long speeches.

'This place'd drive me mad. I'd go bonkers in a week,' he exploded. 'I like life. People. There's plenty of people in the supermarket where I work. That suits me. We'll be having piped music soon. Got to move with the times.'

'And so have I,' said Gibby. 'I've got to think about

supper. Take him round the garden, Miss Lou, if it isn't too dark, and see if you can find any beans. Oh, and bring me in a bunch of parsley, there's a good girl. Take a basket,' she called, as we made for the door, and she started to pile up the tea-things on to a tray. She had certainly done Nigel well. Everything on that table was home-made, and a small jar of her apple jelly stood ready for him to take home.

'Who does all this, then?' asked Nigel grudgingly as we walked over the lawn towards the kitchen garden. The light had not quite gone, and a sullen red glow still lighted up the sky and the garden. 'Big place to keep up.'

'My aunt, the younger one, tries to do what she can. I'm helping while I'm here, and we're trying to get a boy in to do the digging.'

'You living here, then?'

All his questions were gauche, as if he hated to ask them, because they brought him into closer contact. I was reminded of awkward young men on a dance floor.

'No, I've come on a visit, to see how they are.'

We had reached the close-set hedge that hid the kitchen garden and went round it. While I pulled back leaves and searched for the last of the runner beans, Nigel wandered off and looked at everything. He must have noted the unkempt straggle of the raspberries and soft fruit bushes. Then I forgot him in the green sheltered world of beanstalks and leaves. It always brought back that Sunday morning when war was declared. I had been picking beans then, and put up my head to Aunt Seraphina's cry right across the garden, 'War, it's war! Louie, where are you?' as if the very declaration of war over the radio made life outside the house unsafe.

Now I heard another cry. A triumphant one.

'Blackberries! Shall I get a bowl?'

Nigel was down by the barred gate, incongruous in his

dark suit, stripping off blackberries methodically, with a child's greed and pleasure.

'They're so big,' he said, his face open and smiling. 'I've never seen such big ones.'

'Well, do go and get a bowl, we'll pick some for you to take home.'

He was off, with red-stained hands, suddenly years younger, and I was left looking at that barred gate, smothered now with the stranglehold of blackberries. I saw it open, and on the grass, sprawling, a girl's body, with dew shining on her black boots and a slug trail across her face – white as blackberry flowers. I saw an old man, a gardener, turn at the sight of those abandoned black-stockinged legs, to run on his stiff old feet up to the house, there to alarm the cook, busy with breakfast. He had seen dead things in the garden before: rats, nestlings, even a cat. But people, he might have said later to the parlour maid, people should die in their beds.

Looking up, I half expected to see the young, shocked face of Bill Protheroe over the wall. If he hadn't got up late on account of the party, he would have discovered the body, he'd said. But he had seen it and the sight had carried forward, intact, into his extreme old age, and would stay there until death cancelled out the picture and evened things up.

Nigel came back and started to fill the bowl.

'How many d'you want for the house?' he asked:

'We don't eat them,' I told him. Adding, with a small laugh as he prepared to hold this, too, against us. 'That is, it *is* October, isn't it?'

'The fourth,' he spoke as if to an idiot.

'My grandmother used to say that the devil was in blackberries picked after the last day of September. She said they'd been bathed in witches' tears.'

'Witches' what?' he repeated. 'Witches' tears? Cor!

Some of these old wives' tales. Serve you right to go hungry. Get on, don't believe that, do you?'

'Anyway,' I said, evading the question, 'the aunts don't like the pips.' And I picked up my basket of beans and told him he could take as many as he liked. He was welcome.

I left the beans with Gibby, and went through to hang my coat in the hall. Then I stopped dead. My suitcase stood at the foot of the stairs, against the wall. I tried it; it was locked. Then I took the key hanging from the handle by its little chain, and opened it. All my clothes were packed neatly, a piece of tissue-paper spread over the top.

I ran upstairs, to my room. The bed had been stripped. The book that had been beside the bed for so many nights had gone; back to the shelves in the study, I imagined. I looked round the room. The children and the mouse in the picture were once more in possession. To me it was cold and white and impersonal. The zipped-up poodle lay on the folded blankets, flat as a woman after childbirth.

A terrible pain began to throb at the back of my head and I ran out of the room, down one flight of stairs, then another, calling in panic, 'Aunt Seraphina! Aunt Seraphina!'

I took the last bend of the stairs two at a time, and when I saw who was standing in the hall, missed my footing and would have fallen, heavily, absurdly, had not Max run forward and caught me.

TWENTY

'Hush,' said Max, holding me against him tightly. 'It's all right; come in here,' and he half carried me into the morning-room, right across to the love-seat where Aunt Rosa had sat that morning. 'You didn't hurt yourself, did you?'

I shook my head and looked at him.

'Sorry,' I said. 'You gave me a shock, that's all. What are you doing here?'

He was so surprised that he took his arm away and stared.

'I've come to take you home, of course. Didn't you expect me? One of your aunts telephoned last night. I think it was Cissie. She said —'

'Aunt Cissie! She never told me. What did she say?'

'Just that it was time you came home, and would I pick you up this evening. So here I am. I didn't keep the taxi, in case you weren't ready, but we can ring the station to send one.'

I sat quite still. Aunt Cissie again! But someone else must have packed my case. Had Aunt Seraphina known all the time, or had she just been told while I was conveniently out?

'I was going to telephone you tomorrow anyway,' I said. 'Everything's all right now, Max, but —'

'That's fine, then; it'll be nice to have you home. I've painted the flat, by the way, and I've thought of a way to use part of that windfall of yours. *If* you agree.'

I waited, and he went on, 'I thought we might buy a second-hand car and get out to the country at week-ends. Have more fun. Would you like that?'

Sharply, suspiciously, I said, 'You don't have to baby me, Max. Did Aunt Cissie suggest that, too?' But I was only trying to retrieve my self-respect, and Max knew it. 'Where are they all?' I asked.

'Aunt Seraphina let me in, and then scuttled back to your Aunt Cissie's room. They're watching the goggle-box.'

'They don't want me any longer,' I said, full of self-pity.

'Of course not. They never wanted you, really. You wanted them. I —'

'If you say "I told you so" I'll hit you.'

'Carry on, then.' Max did an imitation of a brave man thrusting his chest forward for a blow and waited.

'You're impossible.'

'Darling, of course I am, otherwise I couldn't live with you.'

We kissed, and it was strange in that room to kiss in kindness and love.

'I'd like a glass of sherry, would you?'

Max nodded, and I went out and along to the dining-room to the sideboard, found the key of the tantalus and poured two glasses from one of the three cut-glass decanters. The other two held port and brandy.

We drank in silence, and Max said, 'Well, we'd better go in and say good-bye. That is, if they can tear themselves away long enough. It's a great leveller, the telly. They're in there, one huge dilated eye, taking in everything that's fed to them in measured doses; a laugh, a cry, a moral uplift chat, and democracy verses the rest . . .'

'They're *really* looking at other people, Max. The sort of people who live across the common. They're watching them at last.'

We walked slowly along the corridor, hand in hand. The room that had once been grandfather's study, Sir Roger's place, was bathed in blue light. A table lamp was the only illumination apart from the fire and the emanation from the screen. The three old ladies were shapes in chairs, a glint on spectacles, a shine on hair. They were watching the compére of some variety show: a big, soft, mushy man, who passed himself around the assembled performers like a loving cup. When he turned to beam at his invisible audience it was as if a ripe tomato had been lobbed into one's face.

'Ssh,' hissed Aunt Seraphina. 'Just a moment, dear.'

But Aunt Cissie at once wheeled herself over to the set and turned off the sound.

'You said it was rubbish, Fina,' she said, maliciously, 'So you won't mind if we have it off to say good-bye to Louie.'

'Good-bye?' repeated Aunt Rosa, from her arm-chair. 'What, is she going now? Louie, are you really going?'

Obviously the other two had not told her of their conspiracy, and now they looked uncomfortable. Aunt Seraphina kept looking at the soundless screen, hating to miss what was going on, either there, or in the room. I said calmly, 'Aunt Seraphina was kind enough to pack for me whilst I was out.'

'It came up last night, Rosa, so don't pretend to be surprised,' said Aunt Cissie sharply. 'She's proud, like us. She would never have telephoned.'

'Well,' said Aunt Rosa, with a difficult, bemused little smile. 'And there's Max. I can't see you in this light. Switch on the main one, please. Ah, that's better.' Blinking, she put a hand over her eyes for a moment and gathered herself together. 'Well, we've loved having you, dear. It was very good of you to come, and I do hope —'

'Good of her. It wasn't good at all. Selflessness is non-existent today. I don't believe in it, as you know. I don't believe in goodness, either, I've lived too long. There are motives for every so-called kind action. Like moles under a lawn.'

Max said, quietly, 'You're lucky to have so much self-knowledge, Aunt Cissie,' and she, not understanding the double-edge, smiled as if at a compliment.

'Well, old age is pointless without it, young man. Just as

youth is pointless without idealism. You can add all the other blessings – beauty and enthusiasm and so on – but idealism youth must have.'

'What's she talking about?' asked Aunt Seraphina irritably, 'I thought Gibby was coming in to watch. We don't want to miss all of it. Don't chatter so, Cissie, and don't stand about, you two. Put out the light and sit down.'

I went over and kissed each of my aunts. To Aunt Rosa I said, 'Telephone if you need us. We'll come at once.'

'We shall be all right,' replied Aunt Rosa, 'there's nothing wrong with us, except mortality.'

She pressed my hand and looked once, anxiously, into my eyes. I nodded back my answer. Everything was to be laid away, finally. 'By the way, Louie,' she went on, 'I meant to ask you. I had a letter from that young Mr Bradshaw. He wants to see me, something about shares. I shall have to go up when I'm better.'

'You can take his advice,' I said. 'He'll do his best. Things have changed, Aunt Rosa. Some shares are better than others, and people on fixed incomes —'

'Yes, well, we needn't go into all that now. Do look at Seraphina! Pull yourself together, my girl, Louie's not going for ever.'

For Aunt Seraphina, now that she had freed herself from the gesticulating silent world of the screen by the bed, had at last realized that we were really going, and she was crying. Now she clasped me in her hard, dry way and begged us to stay for supper. Max, who had been looking at the watercolours on the walls, turned at this and said, 'I thought we'd have dinner in town tonight. May I telephone for a taxi?'

While he was out of the room, Aunt Seraphina said, as she had done many times before, 'Remember, dear, this is your home. Come again.'

I didn't contradict her, but I said that next time I would bring Max. Aunt Cissie, who felt she had done her part, now said briskly, 'Call Gibby, Fina, if they're really off. Luckily there's not one of those dreadful plays on tonight – all real life and bad morals. Reality's all right,' she added strongly, 'that is, for some people, but you can't live with it all the time.'

And she tinkled her way over to the television set and turned the knob. Voices at once sprang into the room. 'Switch off the light as you go, Louie.'

None of them turned as I closed the door behind me.

It was Gibby who waved us good-bye from the front door, and I saw her little face screw up as we drove away from The Hollies.

I said, 'They'll quarrel so over the programmes.'

'Quarrels are good for them, they replenish their energy, prove they're still alive,' said Max. 'They don't attack each other's fantasy life. They know when to stop.'

We drove through the long autumn streets; they looked chilly, with a hint of frost and fog. Max spoke again, reflectively:

'Interesting what you can live with, if you've an innocent mind free from twists. It doesn't occur to the old dears that those innocuous watercolours in that room are thumping casebook examples of phallic art. Who did them, Louie? That cuckoo pint. Devilish clever. It's often astonishing to me how skilful Victorian erotica was.'

I sat beside him, holding his hand warmly, and made my last private decision.

'I don't know,' I said. 'We found them in the attic. Some friend of my grandfather's, I expect. Does it matter?'

His silence told me it did not.

'You'll see,' he went on comfortably, moments later. 'They'll be all right now they've Aunt Cissie with them. And her television. They can watch life go by, and it can't intrude. They can keep in touch, but they can control it. Funny thing, Louie: some people are born watchers.

Depends on what side of the fence you are. You either watch, or you create for the watchers. That's what art's about, really. . . .' And he went on expounding this theory all the way to the station. I listened, for it was one of his favourite themes, and now I had no resentment.

I listened and said nothing, although I could have given him living – and dead – proof of his theory. But certain things are best left unsaid; that's the beginning of wisdom. Certain things belong only to the people intimately concerned, and after all, I am still half-Braithwaite, and one cannot betray one's family.